T0277137

DEADPAN

Advance Praise

"Amid a resurgence in global antisemitism and furious identity politics, the nightly scenes of angry mobs and all the grim commentary, we needed a comedic break. *Deadpan* provides a humorous but serious story of an antisemite turned Jewish comedian, reminding us that the most potent—and underused—weapon against bigotry and hate is farce and laughter."

— David Bernstein, author of *Woke Antisemitism*

"The manic, comic energy of Richard Walter's *Deadpan* is so engaging that you may fail to see the serious intent percolating beneath. An ingenious fable of foibles and fallacies across the multiverse."

— Rebecca Newberger Goldstein
author of *Plato at the Googleplex: Why Philosophy Won't Go Away*

"They say satire is what closes on Saturday night. If Richard Walter's *Deadpan* were adapted for the stage, in a production that faithfully preserved its sardonic edge, seriocomic sensibility, metaphysical hijinks, and madly inventive plot twists, it would run till the end of the century."

— James Morrow, author of *The Last Witchfinder*

"I found the book 'breathtaking'…, it literally took my breath away as it moved from one reality to another. I really enjoyed it."
— Rabbi Laura Geller

"In Richard Walter's humorous novel *Deadpan*, a small-town car salesman blinks and opens his eyes to find himself living as one of America's most beloved comedians … The charm and playfulness of the writing has a dual impact. On the one hand, it matches the fun and genuine pleasure of reading an already amusing story. The prose reflects the chaos and evenhanded nonsense of an unpredictable world in a masterful, seamless way. On the other hand, the book takes on some of the most serious of subjects—antisemitism and hate speech … The book is as delightful for its wordplay as it is for its imaginative plot."
— Foreword Reviews

"In this smart satire about bigotry and intolerance, Walter uses magical realism and comedy to reinforce his satirical look at societal problems … This is an intriguing novel that will have readers in stitches."
— U.S. Reviews

DEADPAN

– A Novel –

Richard Walter

UNBOUNDED CREATIVITY
HERESY
PRESS
FEARLESS EXPRESSION

Heresy Press books may be purchased in bulk at special discounts for sales promotion, corporate gifts, fund-raising, or educational purposes. Special editions can also be created to specifications. For details, contact the Special Sales Department, Skyhorse Publishing, 307 West 36th Street, 11th Floor, New York, NY 10018 or info@skyhorsepublishing.com.

Skyhorse Publishing® is a registered trademark of Skyhorse Publishing, Inc.®, a Delaware corporation.

Visit our website at skyhorsepublishing.com.

HERESY PRESS
P.O. Box 425201
Cambridge, MA 02142
heresy-press.com

Heresy Press is an imprint of Skyhorse Publishing.

10 9 8 7 6 5 4 3 2 1

Library of Congress Cataloging-in-Publication Data is available on file.

Jacket design by Elizabeth Cline

Hardcover ISBN: 978-1-949846-64-5
Ebook ISBN: 978-1-949846-65-2

Printed in the United States of America

For Cooper, Magnolia, and Zadie

CHAPTER
I

He switched off the lights, but they continued burning brightly.

Odd, he thought. What do you know about that?

He took a second swipe, but his hand raked air—the switch was gone. Not only the switch, but the green vinyl partition separating his office from the showroom floor. The office furniture, the office, the showroom—all were gone, all but the lights, which now glowed more brightly than before. Glowed, heck. White hot, they seared his retinas, and he slammed his eyelids.

Darndest thing.

Eyes jammed tight, Bridges denied everything. This isn't happening; that's all there is to that. In another moment, he should open his eyes to find the dealership intact, previously owned models gleaming outside on the lot beneath the web of raw globes, latest models—newly delivered '74s—secure within the showroom.

Traffic on Old Deerfield would continue hissing past.

What the hey, he thought. While my eyes are closed, and since I'm dreaming anyway, why not have some fellow wander in and order up a fleet of Skylarks or Electras or whatever? Not necessarily a big fleet; a modest fleet would do. But then, Buicks never were too big a fleet type of vehicle, God alone knows why. With your Buick, Bridges ruminated, it's strictly your old one-at-a-time.

And in normal times, one-at-a-time was enough.

But these were not normal times.

He opened his eyes, then shut them again quickly. Everything was the same, which is to say everything was different.

The dealership was still plainly missing.

There was only harsh, blinding light.

Even with his eyes tightly sealed, however, Bridges could take comfort in the meager available data. First off, this isn't blindness. Blindness is darkness, blackness, and this is the opposite of that.

This is all white, pure linen white.

That's first off.

Second off, as he allowed one eye to open the narrowest slit, he could see that he could see. And what he saw was not merely light but lights.

He saw the word *Sylvania* and the number *100* followed by the letter *W*. Land sakes alive, here was a light bulb, plain as day.

And here was another, and another and another, all of them forming a too-bright rectangle framing an image of a face—a familiar face—squinting back at him. What was familiar about the face, Bridges realized after studying it for a generous beat, was that it was his own. Its features weren't similar, they were identical—strong, straight nose, high cheekbones, close-set gray eyes.

A distinguished American face.

There was only one difference.

Dwight Bridges was achingly, glaringly bald. Here and now, however, he sported a glorious tangle of locks. Obviously a wig,

Bridges figured. He reached up and tugged at the follicles in a futile attempt to liberate the contrivance from his scalp. Must be glued solid to the skin, he thought. Bridges ran his fingers through the mop, picking the strands apart. He concluded this was the goods. Somehow he had acquired an authentic head of hair.

What's more, his drab cord pants were gone, also his folksy flannel shirt and ratty lambswool crewneck sweater. Instead, he wore a maroon tuxedo, black bow tie, and a powder-blue ruffled silk shirt.

As his gaze migrated to his reborn hairline, which featured a modest widow's peak, one of the bulbs flickered, then blew with a gentle metallic ping. This is a mirror, he realized. A God-blessed mirror with lights all around the perimeter, like backstage at a theater in some backstage-at-a-theater movie like, say, *All About Eve*, which he'd caught late one night on Hoggzswallow Hollow's one and only TV station—foggy, fuzzy UHF Channel 34.

He had paid scant attention to the movie, actually dozing during the brief snatches of drama separating commercials. It was the commercials, after all, that interested him. He would perk up wide awake as they flashed across the screen. On his ruled yellow pad, he would take notes as he monitored his competition, gloating but also despairing over the woeful nature of the ads.

Fair is fair, and Bridges appreciated his adversaries were churchgoing Christians, but as to whether or not they were sincerely God-fearing, well, he had his doubts. Now and again, most notably in their commercials with their clowns, costumes, and confetti, they operated very much in the manner of your typical Hebraic merchant.

And why not? They were crafty businessmen, Bridges acknowledged. You had to give them that. Where your Israelite went, so went his influence; there were millennia of testimony to the fact.

The problem was that they had no sense of honor.

He could hold his own against honorable competition, but cutthroat Jewish-style was a different story. Sure, this gasoline crunch, this purported recession, all these factors had to account at least in part for the sales slump at Bridges Buick. But there were, Bridges knew, deeper, darker reasons too. These concerned the waning of faith, the swarthy, brooding influence of a mentality and culture in its essence alien to your Free Enterprise System, your American Way.

To say such things out loud these days was hardly politic, so Bridges confined himself mainly to muttering.

And right here and now he muttered, dipping a powder puff into a cylindrical box of flesh-colored dust, neutral pancake make-up, patting his cheekbones and forehead, trying to dampen the hot spots gleaming back at him from the mirror in such a fashion as to remind him of his unsold cars.

Lord in Heaven have mercy on my soul, he said to nobody. I'm painting my face like some sort of queer.

He would have jumped up and exclaimed "What the hey!" but was distracted by a heavy pounding at the door and an anxious voice.

"Five minutes, Mr. Ritchie! Five minutes!"

What in holy heck is going on here? he wondered.

As his irises adjusted to the up-close bulbs on the dressing-table mirror, he was able to scan the rest of the chamber. Sink. Shower. Metal folding chair on which he sat. Easy chair nearby against one cinder-block wall. Comfy old overstuffed couch against another.

In a minute, Rod Serling shows up, right?

The door flew open and in strode a man distinctly not Rod Serling.

Unlike Serling, for example, he was short and squat. Unlike Serling, he spoke in an anxious, raspy Nu Yawk twang infused with a profound deeze/demz/doze bias. Unlike Serling, he did not offer his customary *Twilight Zone* intro.

Bridges and his mother had caught scattered episodes the previous year, rerun in syndication on Channel 34.

"Yaw most ready, Rich?" the visitor said.

Bridges looked around the cramped quarters in an attempt to discover this Rich fellow, but besides himself, there was nobody.

"Are you talking to me?"

"No, not at all," the man said. "I'm talking to Tricky Dick Nixon. I'm talking to King Fucking Farouk. I'm talking to the man in the moon."

This is getting crazier all the time, Bridges thought. I've simply got to wake up out of this, and in some kind of hurry.

"New?" the man said to Bridges.

Bridges would have said something if he could have thought of something to say, even just a couple of words. In the silence, he became aware for the first time of extraneous, distant sounds, mainly brass. Golly, he thought, there's a band, a pretty hot band, he had to admit, featuring among other instrumentation horns, reeds, and percussion.

These guys sounded darned professional, no doubt about that. Bridges had to hand it to them, whoever and wherever they were.

"Don't play no games with me, please, Richie? No games with your old buddy, Buddy, correct? You got—what?—two minutes before your fanfare, yes? What is it you want? A little eye-opener? A little pick-me-up? A quick snort? Sure, why not? You don't look so hot. You look like you could use a toot."

The man ducked back to the door and threw the deadbolt, sealing—forever, Bridges feared—the two of them in the room. From a pocket inside his jacket he extracted a diminutive glass phial.

He unscrewed the cap.

With a tiny spoon attached to the phial by a delicate silver chain, he dipped into the vessel, withdrawing a tidy hill of fine powder.

Next, he thrust the spoon directly under Bridges's left nostril.

To say this all struck Bridges as curious would constitute the grossest sort of understatement, but it was nothing compared to what the greasy, pockmarked character did next: with his own finger, he clamped shut Bridges's remaining nostril.

"Go!" he commanded.

Bridges brushed the man's hands from his face, sending the spoon and bottle and all of the powder flying.

"Holy Jesus in freaking fucking Heaven, what the freaking fuck are you fucking freaking doing?" the man raged, as if Bridges had run over his wife and kids with an eighteen-wheeler. "Schmuck!" he added. "That was three-hundred bucks' worth of Ecuadorian primo!"

"Now see here," Bridges said. "Just one little moment, if you don't mind." There comes a time in the affairs of men, he reasoned, where no matter how precarious, no matter how perilous the circumstances, a fellow has to assert his authority, stand up for himself, and take responsibility for his actions. This simple precept had resulted in the sale of a heavily loaded Riviera not four months earlier, he recalled.

To be fair, that was before the embargo.

"One little moment is all you got, Rich," Buddy Scheib said to Dwight Bridges, "'cause if my ears don't deceive me, that refrain emanating down the hall is your intro."

Bridges could make out the band playing something upbeat and lusty.

There was a rattling of the doorknob from the other side, and a voice called out, "Time. It's time, Mr. Ritchie. There's your fanfare. You're on."

"Let's just take this one step at a time, Mr. Ritchie," Bridges said to Buddy Scheib.

"Cute, that's cute, Rich. Sure, one step at a time, that's fine by me." Bridges could see that the man—he could only be this Ritchie fellow—was seriously stressed. "One step, and then the next, right?

Is that it? Great. Okay." He yanked back Bridges's chair and, with it, Bridges. "But you can't take a step—can you?—unless first you stand up on your own two feet, yes or no? Yes?" He thrust his arms beneath Bridges's shoulders, attempting to haul him erect.

Never altogether comfortable with physical contact, especially among men, Bridges shoved Scheib back. "Keep your hands off me," he warned.

"Well, for Christ's sake, Richie. Well, for Christ's sake."

"I don't know who you are or what sort of crazy game you're playing," Bridges said. "And I don't even know, for that matter, how I come to be here, wherever 'here' may happen to be. Nevertheless, I'm certain there's a logical explanation that will make itself known presently. Until such time, you shall refrain from touching me. Do you understand?"

"What is this? New material? Save it for your act, Richie. Save it for the paying customers. For now, get your fucking buns on stage. Your worshipful public awaits."

"I haven't the faintest idea what you're talking about."

"Oy gevalt," Scheib said to the ceiling. "Guttenyu!"

In the background, the band was now anxiously marking time, vamping, stalling.

The man began signaling with his fingers and hands, eagerly gesticulating in the manner of American Sign Language, the visual-gesture code designed for the hard-of-hearing, with its own semantic and syntactic structure.

Bridges looked on in confusion. "What are you doing?"

"You don't recognize the band out there playing your theme? I figured maybe you've gone deaf."

"What the fuck's going on?" came a new voice from outside. "Richie? You in there? Scheib?"

Acutely distressed, Buddy Scheib wobbled over toward Bridges. Through a sea of saliva he whispered, "You roused Mr. Big himself, putz. The guy has this funny idea that for his quarter-mill a week, he's entitled to, maybe, an appearance from you, that's all, that you flash your popular punim in front of the paying customers, so they'll know the colossal billboard out front on the boulevard isn't stone bullshit."

"Is anybody in there, goddamnit?" came the voice. The door now rattled so violently that Bridges expected it to disintegrate in a shower of sawdust.

"Right, right, Mr. Avakian," Scheib called out. "Richie's here, ready to roll." He shot a frantic glance at Bridges, then twisted the deadbolt. The door flew open, and a broad-shouldered man in an immaculate custom black tuxedo, virtually identical to Bridges's maroon version, burst into the chamber.

"If this is some kind of cheap-ass scheme to hold me up for more money, you got another think coming, the both of you," he said.

Bridges addressed the man directly. "Excuse me. You are Mr. Avakian, I take it? Do I have that right?"

Avakian stared at Bridges, then turned to Scheib. "He was a bum, a nobody, playing toilets. Who was the first idiot to book him into a big room? Tell me that. What is he trying to pull here? Are you in on this?"

"Nobody's pulling nothing, Mr. A.," Scheib said. "Richie likes to clown around. Right, Rich?"

"Mr. Avakian—I trust I'm getting the pronunciation correct—I wonder if I could have a word with you privately." If only he could ditch this intruder for two seconds, Bridges was certain he could straighten everything out.

"Sure, a word. We'll have plenty of words, privately or on network television or however you like, but after your goddamn set, not before. What about it? In another minute I'm gonna have a fucking riot on my hands. We're talking pitchforks and torches."

I've got to get away, Bridges decided. I've simply got to get out of here. This one's Avakian. That one's Scheib. Who's this Richie character they keep talking about? It's some kind of conspiracy, and they're all in on it. What's clear is I've got to get out of here.

"All right, you scum-humping, thieving, lowlife motherfuckers," Avakian surrendered. "You got me over a frigging barrel, I admit it. I'll give you a thousand a night more. Just get on stage. Now."

In the distance, beyond the thumping, thundering band, was the sound of hands rhythmically clapping, feet stamping, and voices chanting: "Richie! Richie! Richie! Richie!"

"Thousand a set," Buddy Scheib shot back. "Not per night. Per set." He looked over at Bridges. "Right, Rich?" He turned back to face the big man. "That's two thou per night, three each Fridays and Saturdays."

"Right, right," Avakian grumbled. "A set."

If I'm going to get out of here, Bridges reasoned, the first step is to get out of this chair.

He rose to his feet.

"Wait," Scheib admonished Bridges, pushing him back down. This struck Bridges as curious since until now Scheib had been urging him—via moral suasion and sheer physical force—to stand.

"Cash," Scheib said. "My client requires cash. Now."

"Sweet, dear, precious baby Jesus," Avakian said, reaching into his pocket. "For this upcoming set," he groaned, peeling off ten crisp one-hundred dollar bills. He handed them to Scheib, who stuck one in his shiny jacket and tucked the remainder inside Bridges's vest pocket.

"All right, move it now," Avakian said.

Grateful to vacate the premises, Bridges stood up and followed Scheib out the door and into a dark, narrow passage.

At least I'm getting out of here, Bridges thought as they moved toward a wall of light at the end of the corridor. Anything to get out of here. With each step, the music grew louder. It was evident that beyond the brightness there were people, lots of people. And where there were people, Bridges reassured himself, there was help, no doubt about that.

Popping in and out of focus against the light stood a stagehand in shirtsleeves. He looked back toward the approaching trio and shrugged anxiously.

Avakian nodded.

Shirtsleeves seized a telephone wired to a control panel on the wall.

"Cue Richie's theme," he said into the phone, grabbing a fistful of switches, levers, and knobs, flicking, sliding, and rotating them. The light wall fluctuated in intensity and hue. The band quit its endless vamp and retreated to its original motif. As the party arrived at Shirtsleeves's side, Bridges could hear past the music to a burgeoning roar, a sound at once familiar and strange, like surf, like fire, like wind.

Bridges now recognized it as applause.

Both Avakian and Scheib came to a halt at the edge of the light. Neither objected as Bridges sailed past them, out into the luminescence. "Break a leg, Richie," Scheib called after him.

"Lucky I don't break his fucking head," Avakian grumbled under his breath.

"Ladies and Gentlemen," oozed a voice as rich as gelato from a thousand loudspeakers.

The applause grew still more spirited, the reception more clamorous.

Bridges could barely see beyond the harsh light beaming down on him.

Shading his eyes with his hand, he made out various members of the orchestra, in particular the horn players and trombonists, their instruments glinting gold, off to one side of the raised platform on which he found himself standing.

In the harsh glare, squinting, he could hardly see the audience.

In the first row, occupying an upholstered V.I.P. banquette, he spotted Mohammad Reza Pahlavi, Queen Farah, and several members of their security detail. To Bridges at this time, of course, the Shah and his bride were total strangers.

"Ladies and Gentlemen," the voice boomed again, nearly inaudible above the commotion. "The fabulous Starshine Dome of the phenomenal Desert Goliath Hotel, Country Club, Resort, Spa, and Casino proudly presents … Richie Ritchie!"

Ritchie, this Ritchie character, Bridges thought. In a moment he would actually have a look at the guy. Still shading his eyes, Bridges made his way carefully toward the platform's edge. Applause washed over him, accompanied by wild cheering, whistling, hooting, and stamping feet.

The ovation drowned out even the amplified music.

Bridges arrived at the edge of the stage, then moved laterally up and back several steps in each direction, trying to elude the spotlights tracking him wherever he turned. The beams found their target, settling upon all five foot eight inches of him. He dodged left, feinted right, but the light clung to him like Velcro. The scene resembled one of those over-the-wall black-and-white prison-breakout movies from Warner Brothers with actors like James Cagney and Edward G. Robinson, maybe *Angels with Dirty Faces*, which he and his mother had caught one night on Channel 34.

Now, mixing into the cacophony, he could hear a new sound: laughter. Scores of people, hundreds of people, were howling with laughter.

Laughter, of all things, seemed inappropriate to Bridges's predicament, but if there were hundreds, make that thousands of people laughing just beyond the blackness, there also had to be solid citizens who could surely assist him, enlighten him as to what was going on, and advise him as to how he might extricate himself from this most dreadful of nightmares.

"Excuse me, please," he said to the darkness seething before him, but his voice was swallowed by the commotion. "Please, excuse me, please," he said more loudly but still not loudly enough. Even if he cupped his hands and shouted at the top of his lungs, he realized, there was no way to be heard above the din.

He noticed now for the first time, just beyond the circle of light following him everywhere, a gridded cylindrical metal object, a microphone mounted atop a chrome pole. He moved over to it, and the light moved with him. As Bridges stepped up to the mic, the band suddenly ceased playing.

Not quite so abruptly, the cheering and applause subsided.

Bridges tapped the microphone and scratched tentatively at the grid. The tapping crashed like timpani; the scratching resounded like machine-gun fire.

Now, all at once, the room was filled with a gaping, yawning silence.

"Hello, hello," Bridges called into the microphone. His voice screeched back at him at a trillion decibels, causing him to recoil. Reacting to his surprise, there arose among the crowd a mass chuckle.

"I don't know exactly how to explain this," Bridges said, "but something very strange appears to be going on."

There was the thump of a bass drum, a flurry of snare, a cymbal crash, and a rim shot.

"I suppose I should introduce myself," Bridges said.

Already he was becoming adept at working the mic. He knew better now just where to position his lips. He was also becoming accustomed to hearing his voice thunder back at him, even as he spoke in a near whisper.

"My name is Bridges," he explained, trying to sound at once casual and concerned. As if on cue, the laughter swelled, frothed, and licked at his ankles like breakers at the shore. "Dwight Bridges." And then, inexplicably, with his next utterance, the audience commenced talking along with him, in virtual unison, as if they already knew what he would say. "I'm an automobile dealer from Hoggzswallow Hollow, West Virginia."

"... obile dealer from Hoggzs Hoggzswallow zswallow wallow, West Virginia, gin ya, gin ya ya ...," the audience echoed in the cavernous showroom.

Now there was a rising crescendo of laughter and a storm of beating palms. The audience rose to its feet, five thousand cheering acolytes. Their affection rained down upon Bridges in a monsoon of adoration.

The clamor made it impossible for Bridges to continue, even with the microphone, so he stood there, feeling strange, feeling awkward, waiting for the tide to ebb, wondering what in holy heck to do.

Notwithstanding the crowd, he felt wretchedly alone.

As the screams quieted to murmurs, Bridges said, "I don't get it." Even so simple, so natural a sentiment appeared to incite among the congregation a renewed demonstration of approval.

Bridges remained at the microphone.

A numbing calm now settled over him like fog over the West Virginia hill country at night.

"Now listen," he insisted. "I don't know what's going on here, but I'll say this: I'm a human being, and as a human being I'm entitled to a certain amount of courtesy, a modicum of respect, the plain and simple, day-to-day good manners individuals provide one another in a civilized society."

Not a bad little impromptu speech, Bridges thought.

With his fans rocking the room in reborn adulation, Bridges experienced the slightest rush of pleasure.

Humanity, when you get right down to it, is humanity. There's goodness in the worst of us, Bridges reassured himself. A man alone, a man in difficulty, doesn't have to go very far before somebody shows up to offer a helping hand.

Acknowledging, perhaps even welcoming the balmy shelter of the audience's affection, Bridges prattled on in this fashion, stuttering and stammering in fits and starts for another fifteen minutes.

At last, running low on language, unable to invent anything else to say, he turned and headed toward the wings. As he retreated, the band launched an upbeat vamp with the brass blaring double time.

"Gorgeous!" crowed Buddy Scheib upon Bridges's arrival backstage. "Beautiful!"

Scheib! The ordeal had been almost endurable, perhaps even enjoyable these past several moments, if only for allowing Bridges to forget this rodent. He pushed past Scheib but ran flat into Avakian. The big man grasped Bridges's collar with an outstretched arm, a maneuver that reminded Bridges of a deep-water-rescue approach he had learned in Red Cross Senior Lifesaving at the Hoggzswallow Hollow YMCA's indoor pool.

"Listena the crowd," cheered Shirtsleeves. "Never heard nothing like it. Not Wayne Newton. Not Tony Orlando and Dawn bring down the house, create such a racket. Ain't that the truth, Mr. A?"

"They want another look," Avakian said. "We gotta give them another look, or they'll burn the joint to the ground." He seized Bridges's shoulders, pivoted him, and shoved him back out again into the light.

Dwight Bridges, Hoggzswallow Hollow car dealer, stumbled back onto the stage.

The band stepped up the tempo. On sight of him, the audience rose once again to its feet. As Bridges made his tenuous way center, the reception's intensity threatened to rend the very walls.

Even the Shah and his entourage stood, smiling broadly, eagerly applauding.

With the band sprinting, the audience whooping and whistling, Bridges could not help but proffer a half smile.

For a moment he let the safe, salty love rain down upon him.

And then he surprised himself completely.

He took an awkward little bow.

CHAPTER
2

B ridges switched off the lights, and Old Deerfield went dark.
Not all of Old Deerfield, naturally, just that portion fronting the dealership. The streetlamps still hummed—at least every third one, since in compliance with national policy, the township had cut back. Said policy was a dad-blamed mistake, Bridges believed, and Hoggzswallow Hollow's complicity lamentable.

There was even talk of establishing a federal speed limit.

Just imagine some bureaucrat in Washington telling a guy in, say, Idaho, how fast—more accurately, how slow—he could drive. What's more, rumor had it they planned to set the cap at fifty-five.

Fifty-five, for your basic Buick, was like driving in reverse.

Heck, they were making noises about prohibiting merchants from utilizing exterior lighting, at least until the so-called crisis passed. But is not life, Bridges wondered, one ongoing crisis? You don't stack the odds in your favor shunning risk, playing your hand too close to your chest. Isn't that just a fancy way to describe cowardice? The Ay-rabs want to keep their fuel all for themselves? Let's burn ours ten times more brightly. Let them see the beacon of our spirit shining. You certainly don't move automobiles, or any other commodity, if the purchasing public can't tell you're open for business.

Normally an apprentice salesman, one of his commission people, accompanied Bridges on this final inspection tour, shutting down the dealership for the night. It had been something of a ritual, a ceremony, maybe even a Sacrament. Now, however, by necessity having taken the fellows off salary, with compensation based exclusively upon sales, no one stayed past eight.

Bridges couldn't blame them. For several weeks he had moved only a handful of "transportation" vehicles, clunkers well past their prime, secondhand jalopies held together by duct tape and Elmer's Glue.

Didn't they have families to support?

Still, Bridges was disappointed.

What had become of old-fashioned perseverance?

And how about loyalty?

Bridges left a single forty-watter burning outside. Within the showroom, a lone fluorescent cast a pall the color of skim milk. He picked up his battered leather coronet case and went out back to his LeSabre. He climbed in and rolled away.

Even at this hour it looked like at least a ninety-minute wait at the only open station, Bull Donner's Sohio Service, junction of Old Deerfield and New Old Deerfield. Bridges glided slowly past the long line and shook his head woefully. He turned right and continued toward his destination.

A mile or so down the road, he passed Dale Dixon's Datsun Depot. Bridges ruefully observed the dealership's lights burning brightly. Passing the showroom, in his rearview mirror Bridges could make out sales personnel mingling with customers as they scrutinized the merchandise.

After another couple of miles, Bridges pulled up in front of Ezra Convy's pitch-black Mobil.

There was not a soul in sight.

He tapped a quick, quiet honk.

After a moment, the service panel door rose.

Ezra hurried out. "Can't fill you," he said. "Are you empty? Can't fill you."

"I drove up here, didn't I? I'm almost empty, but obviously I'm not empty."

"Kill your lights. Let's get this over with quick enough, okay? We don't want folks looking on, getting suspicious. We don't want to call attention to ourselves, most especially tonight." He unscrewed the cap, shoved in the nozzle, and squeezed the handle.

"What's so special about tonight?" Bridges asked.

"Sell you five gallons," Convy said, ignoring the question. "Call it a quarter tank."

"Ez, I'm grateful."

"God helps those what et cetera."

"You scratch my hand," Bridges said, "I'll wash your back, or however that goes."

"Exactly." Convy pronounced it *egg-zackly*.

The sound of fuel sloshing into his tank soothed Bridges at the same time as it troubled Convy. One was getting, the other giving. "There's five," Convy said to Bridges as the wheels spun on the gas pump's gauge. Surprisingly, Convy did not shut it off, but kept pumping. "Give you six, Dwight, and we'll use your car tonight."

"Use my car for what?"

"You'll know soon enough," Convy whispered conspiratorially, as if someone might overhear, as if the two of them were not alone in the West Virginia night.

"That's fair, long as we're not going eight miles, city. Eight miles, city," Bridges said, "brings me back down to five gallons, which is where I started."

"We're not going no eight miles," Convy assured him. "No eight miles. Well, barely."

He shut off the pump and signaled to Bridges to bring his car into the bay. "Looks funny parked here at the pumps. People get curious. These days the land is awash in mistrust."

"Isn't that the sorry truth?" Bridges said, easing the vehicle forward.

He turned off the motor and climbed out of the car.

Convy let the service-bay door slide back down.

Inside, Warren Robertson and both Baker brothers were present, the music stands set up in the adjacent bay. Greetings were traded as Bridges removed the case, opened the lid, and withdrew the horn and mouthpiece. He fit one into the other, then blew a couple of sloppy arpeggios. Now he sat down in the folding chair before the stand. He opened the spiral-bound thousand-tune fake book to the appropriate chart.

Convy settled his ample buttocks onto the cutoff bar stool amidst his drums. He twirled the sticks, dropping one, which hit the poured-concrete floor with a hollow click. He picked it up, then rapped hard on the tom-tom.

"Short jam tonight, boys. Got work to do, right?"

All nodded, except for Bridges.

"Work?" Bridges asked. "Precisely what sort of work?"

"That's all decided. We decided while waiting for you. You wanna be in on the deciding, you gotta show up at rehearsal on time," Curtis Baker, the younger of the brothers, told Bridges.

"Yeah, sure, but I can't close my place till ten."

"You can close your place anytime you damn want, Dwight. You own the joint, don't you? You're the boss."

"Which is exactly why I can't shut down whenever I feel like it. Thanks to the crisis, I've already cut back my hours."

"Cut back more," Warren Robertson said as he tested the keys on his clarinet. "I drive past your place eight-thirty and don't see exactly no crowd in your showroom."

"Business is bad all around, Warren," Curtis Baker said in Bridges's defense. "This gas thing ain't no kinda boon to Dwight's operation, wouldn't you say? He cuts back any further, bound to look like he's caving in to 'conservation' or 'regulation' or whatever the so-called experts call it in DC." He plucked his upright bass, then rotated the peg for the bottom E, tuning the string down a quarter step.

"Don't have to tell me about no gas thing," Convy said. "This here's a gas station, right?"

"Gas thing or no gas thing," Bridges said, "we don't triumph over it by slamming commerce to a halt, do we?"

"Okay, okay, all right. We're all here to do something about it, to take action, instead of just flapping our jaws. Isn't that what we're doing here?"

"We are gonna play, aren't we?" the older Baker said. "I mean, we are gonna play." He teased a few notes from the off-pitch spinet, which looked out of place backed against the wall of a gas station's service bay.

"Naturally. We're gonna play till eleven and thirty," Convy said, "just like any Tuesday. Then we go out and do what has to be done." He rapped a riff on his hi-hat, then said, "One, two, and ..."

They leaped into a sour but exuberant "Saints," prominently featuring Bridges, with Warren Robertson jabbing impromptu forays against the melody.

From "Saints" they went to "House of the Rising Sun," then onto "Saint James Infirmary" and "Twelfth Street Rag" and the rest of the timeworn repertoire they'd gleaned from old seventy-eights and tattered sheet music.

To Albert Morrow, alone in the first house up Walnut off New
Old Deerfield, it sounded dreadful. True, he had to strain to hear
at all, had to crank up his hearing aid, had to cock his head at a
curious angle, which made him look like his mixed-breed spaniel.
Still, he was entitled to peace. The racket represented to him no
mere annoyance but a brazen trampling of his rights as a citizen,
stakeholder, taxpayer, homeowner, and human American being.

He'd stopped phoning the cops months back when he realized
they were only humoring him. He'd learned that they'd even or-
ganized an informal Tuesday-night pool at headquarters in which
the officer guessing the time closest to Morrow's call took home
the pot.

Most nights it ran to three or four dollars.

Eventually, after a weary reprise of "Saints," Ezra Convy pointed to his watch.

"Eleven and a half, gents," he said. "Zero hour."

"Oh, shove the *Mission: Impossible* lingo and let's get on with it,"
said young Baker.

"Get on with what?" Bridges asked.

"If you was here per schedule," Warren Robertson said, disas-
sembling his clarinet, "you'd know."

"Just hush and you'll see soon enough," Convy said, fiddling
with a Pioneer H-R100 eight-track stereo player he'd stripped
from a wrecked '55 Pontiac Star Chief. "Just let me set this up, and
we'll move on to the task at hand."

Ezra ran wires from the device to twin terminals on the station's
battery charger. He connected two oversize KLH-6 speakers, then
jammed a *Best of Dixieland* anthology cassette into the slot.

Satch's horn wailing "Ain't Misbehavin'," flooded the bay.

Not exactly Dixie, Bridges thought from his standpoint as a
purist, but worthy nonetheless. With Pops, you never go wrong.

Ezra turned up the volume way too loud then went over to the
cinder-block sidewall and opened a window.

"That oughta do it, don't you think?"

Bridges couldn't figure what it was all about, but he was so lost in the magic of Armstrong's artistry that he didn't care. The instrumental lead-in ended; the gritty, phlegm-drenched vocal began.

Convy flicked a switch and the massive door rose. Bridges eased his car outside into the November night, and the door slid shut behind him, only slightly muffling the jazz.

The others boarded the LeSabre.

"Do I get a clue?" Bridges asked from behind the wheel.

"Turn right. Take Old North to Emerson Highway and follow toward town," Convy instructed.

Bridges moved the car out onto the road, and they slipped through the sleeping village. It was a soundless world, except for the pebbles or marbles or ball bearings or whatever they were rattling in the cans that the boys passed around among themselves.

"What's this?" Bridges asked as he was handed one of his own.

"What's it look like?" said Convy. "A cow chip? An alarm clock? A French poodle? It's a can of paint. Spray paint. You got to agitate; says so right here on the label. Guess you could call us agitators."

One of the Bakers, Bridges wasn't sure which, joined with Robertson and Convy in dark laughter. "Yeah, agitators. That's us."

"But what for?" said Bridges.

"To keep it solvent or something, I guess," Convy explained, rattling the canister of red engine primer. "They put some kinda something in there so when you shake it, it stirs things up."

"Stir things up is what we're about this evening, gents," Robertson said.

"It's a good thing I love a mystery," Bridges said.

"You'll see soon enough what we're up to, Dwight. Just make sure you don't drip paint on your clothes. That would provide evidence for law enforcement, should they get curious."

"Evidence?" Bridges asked. "Law enforcement?"

"Not to worry," Convy said. "Cops got bigger fish to fry. It's unlikely they'd get involved. To play it safe though, once we're done, lose the canister. If the authorities start sniffing around, it could connect you to tonight's adventure."

"Authorities?" Bridges asked. "Adventure?"

The questions went unanswered.

The car drove left, right, and straight ahead, with Convy directing where Bridges should turn. Against his better judgment, Bridges pretended there was a raw egg between his foot and the accelerator pedal, the sort of gas-saving measure he'd heard some government genius recommend on talk radio. Seemed stupid to him, operating a five-thousand-dollar upholstered, air-conditioned chariot in such a fashion as to conserve a nickel's worth of gas. Organizing so monumental an achievement in automotive engineering around a thimbleful of fuel, well, right there was what had gone wrong with America.

"Kill the lights, then head up this here driveway."

Bridges performed as instructed. The car came to a halt behind a darkened twenty-four-hour-grocery outlet. As a sign indicated, in compliance with the new federal energy guidelines, it had closed.

"This the place?" said one of the Bakers.

"No, but it oughta be. We oughta fix all these cringing bastards what caves in to the bureaucrats and despoilers." The angrier Convy grew, the more crackery his syntax, the more down-homey his vernacular.

They sat quietly in the car ten full minutes.

"Coast's as clear as she'll ever be," Convy announced at last. "Let's get to it, what say?"

They eased the doors open and stepped out of the car. Convy led the team past the darkened store and down an alley running behind several adjacent structures. They arrived at last in the parking lot behind Congregation B'Nai Ohev Shalom.

Silent as Vietcong, they crept around to the main entrance. Ezra snapped off the cap from his cylinder, rattled one last rattle, looked to his compatriots, shrugged, then turned to face the double oaken doors. As the others watched, wielding his spray canister, he painted a broad red swastika.

Cans at the ready, the group fanned out around the synagogue.

"Burn Jews Not Oil," wrote Warren Robertson in fat, dripping letters along the north brick wall.

"Hitler Was Right," young Baker scrawled, not quite illegibly, on the pavement of a patio.

Out back, older Baker drew another Nazi twisted cross, but the paint ran and it came out looking like a pair of squared-off eights standing side by side.

Now he painted the legend, "Deport Jewish Scum."

Then he turned to Bridges, who stood there numb, can in hand.

"What about it?" he said.

Bridges shrugged.

"Well?"

Bridges reluctantly flipped the cap on his paint can and pressed the button. A few droplets spit from the nozzle and fell to his shoes.

"Shake it," Ez Convy said. "You have to shake it."

Bridges shook it.

With his index finger still depressing the nozzle, paint spurted. A waft of breeze seized a portion of the spray, carrying it back to his ratty lambswool sweater, and then to the spot where Baker was working.

"Watch it, Dwight, will you? You'll wreck a perfectly fine garment."

"Sorry," Bridges whispered. Could the disheveled older Baker really care about wardrobe, or was he just performing his trademark contrarian routine? "Try benzene," he advised. "Then soak overnight in soapy water. Rinse, repeat, and tumble dry on low heat."

"Well?" Baker said again to Bridges.

Bridges hesitated.

At last, in billowy red script, he painted, "Dump Kissinger."

CHAPTER
3

With the ovation thundering in the background, a cordon of armed security personnel hustled Bridges along the corridor leading to the backstage exit. Outside, there awaited a stretch limo as long as the *Queen Mary*. The door swung open with that costly metallic suck belonging exclusively to Bentley.

Bridges climbed aboard.

The door swung closed behind him.

He sank back into upholstery so plush it swallowed his butt and belly up to his navel.

He sat there alone, in perfect silence.

Now there arose the muffled *thuck-thuck* of a helicopter engine coming to life.

Through a tinted window, Bridges observed at the edge of the parking lot a heavyweight chopper, a military-grade twin-rotor

CH-47 Chinook, painted in the tan-and-brown paisley design characteristic of desert camouflage.

Its rotors were just now beginning to turn.

Emblazoned across its body was a legend written in a script that, to Bridges, was alien.

Arabic? Hindi? Sindhi? Farsi? Urdu? Punjabi?

Bridges knew it was not Hebrew.

He knew that because a year earlier, maybe two, Pastor Pete had invited a scriptural-Hebrew scholar to preach to the congregation at Mt. Zion Baptist Assembly of God. So many parishioners, the pastor lamented, claim to revere the literal word of God when, in fact, they have never read the literal word of God.

They have read, he declared, a translation.

In the parking lot, the rotors picked up speed. Soon enough, the craft lifted precariously from the tarmac, wobbling just a bit in midair, then stabilizing and finally disappearing into the clouds.

In the limousine, a telephone purred.

Bridges scanned the vehicle's interior. He discovered a retro receiver fashioned from hand-carved ivory wired to a state-of-the-art control panel reminiscent of the high-tech light board backstage at the showroom he had just exited.

He picked up the receiver.

"Music, Mr. Ritchie?" a voice inquired.

Bridges stared curiously at the receiver.

"It is I, sir," the voice explained patiently. "Henry, your driver. Will you have some music?"

Bridges looked forward a bowling-alley's length to the driver's compartment. Peering back at him through a window of smoked glass, a uniformed chauffeur held a phone to his ear.

"Music?" Bridges asked.

"Name your pleasure," the chauffeur said. "Folk? Rock? Folk rock? Pop? Protest? Middle-of the-road? Tongan choral? Album-oriented contemporary? Cool jazz? Hot jazz? Progressive jazz?"

Jazz made Bridges think of Dixieland, and Dixieland brought to mind Ez Convy, Warren Robertson, and a couple of Baker brothers. But instead of asking for jazz, Bridges heard himself say, "Classical."

"Excellent," Henry the chauffeur said. "Symphonic or chamber? Perhaps a string quartet?"

Bridges grunted his assent. "Whatever."

"Fair enough," Henry said. "We'll go with chamber music."

A limo door opened.

Four showgirls boarded.

Each wore a G-string, pale-blue tasseled pasties, and flecked-and-speckled stilettos with three-inch spiked heels. The first carried a cello; another held a viola; the remaining pair toted violins.

With an electric hum, four jump seats unfolded from panels beneath the velvet carpeting.

The musicians settled into the chairs.

"I'm Arlene, Mr. Ritchie," said the cellist. She turned to the violist. "She's Darlene." Now she indicated the fiddle players. "This is Charlene," she said, "and that's Marlene."

"Actually, I'm Marlene," said the first violinist. Pointing to her colleague holding the other violin, she said, "She's Charlene."

"What'll you have, Mr. Ritchie?" Arlene inquired. "Mozart? Brahms? Scriabin? Zappa?"

The limousine stirred; Bridges perceived that the vehicle was now in motion.

"It's all the same to me," he told the women.

The musicians looked at each other, inhaled a collective breath, nodded in unison, and launched Borodin's Quartet no. 8 in C Minor Op. 110. Bridges was immediately caught up in the swaying of the tassels as the players shifted in their seats, and also in their exceptional virtuosity.

Not eight measures into the first movement, the vehicle and the music came to a halt.

The door popped open, and the chauffeur stood at attention outside, holding the platinum door handle. "We've arrived, Mr. Ritchie."

He reached out a hand to Bridges.

The limo sat idling opposite an entrance to the same high-rise hotel from which they had emerged only moments earlier. Bridges allowed himself to be helped to the pavement.

"But they only just started playing," he told the driver.

"They should be delighted to continue, sir," Henry said, "if that is your desire."

Bridges's desire, even in the fog of what he took to be an ongoing series of cascading delusions, was to get home to Hoggzswallow Hollow, back to his failing but familiar Buick dealership. The first step toward that goal, he determined, was to shake off all those who had intruded upon his life.

Chauffeur Henry withdrew from his jacket not one but two gleaming silver keys. He plunged each into recessed slots in the hotel's raked stucco wall. He cranked them a quarter turn. This was succeeded by an electrical hum and subtle meshing of gears. A portion of the wall slid away, revealing a confined yet sumptuous chamber, not much larger than an oversized phone booth.

Like a matador flourishing a phantom cape, with a sweeping gesture the chauffeur ushered Bridges and the women inside.

The wall panel slid closed behind them.

Crammed together with the players, their instruments, and their horsehair bows, Bridges reckoned he had trespassed into territory where he did not belong. He studied the chamber's innards. Its walls were upholstered in quilted fur. Honest to God mink or sable or beaver or ermine or otter or seal or something, Bridges speculated. None of your acrylic or rayon or whatever, as one finds among Buick's interior options.

The floor, Bridges noted, was red-oak parquet.

"Good thing I didn't request, say, Mahler's Third, requiring an entire orchestra," Bridges quipped, imagining a hundred players and their gear, all of them crammed into these tight quarters. "Or Beethoven's Ninth," he added, "with all that, plus a hundred-voice chorus."

The women responded with forced guffaws.

"An entire orchestra!" Darlene clucked.

"Plus their instruments!" Charlene chuckled.

"And a hundred-voice chorus!" Arlene chortled.

"Oh, that's marvelous!" Arlene gushed. "Isn't that hilariously marvelous?" she asked the others.

"It is," said Marlene. "Hilariously marvelous and marvelously hilarious!"

Bridges wanted to believe that they were sincere, but he sensed a certain condescension.

The door slid open

Before them now stood neither the chauffeur nor auxiliary entrance to the hotel, but a full-floor penthouse luxury suite. Next to these digs, the Taj Mahal was a Bronx tenement walkup.

Cautiously, Bridges and the women stepped out of the elevator to find their feet swallowed in ankle-deep pile. They wandered timidly into a sunken living room featuring, through floor-to-ceiling windows, an Ultra-Panavision view of the Vegas skyline. Beyond the Strip's garish neon lay the surrounding desert, its purple mountains looming.

"I heard of it," Darlene whispered to her colleagues, scanning the premises in shock and awe. "I heard it described by some of the girls, but I never saw it with my own eyes."

"He has girls up here?" asked Arlene.

"He's a man, right?" Darlene said.

"I know a dancer at the Sands who knows a waitress at the Dunes who knows a blackjack dealer who knows somebody who

knows somebody," Charlene said. "They keep it a big secret, naturally, like everything else about him."

"About whom?" Bridges asked.

"Why, Mr. Pahlavi, of course," Darlene said, whispering the
name so quietly, Bridges wasn't certain he'd caught it correctly.
"The sultan or caliph or emir or mullah or imam or whatever they
call him. Rajah, maybe. Aga. Pasha. Something like that."

"Shah," Marlene said.

"That's the guy!" Darlene said. "They evicted him from this suite
earlier today to make it available to you, Mr. Ritchie. But surely you
know that. Your manager, Buddy Scheib, told us you insisted these
particular digs be written into your contract with the showroom."

"Ladies," Arlene gently reprimanded, "perhaps Mr. Ritchie
doesn't care to hear a lot of girly claptrap and would like us to
resume playing."

"What I would like," Bridges said, thoroughly surprising himself, "is a nice, hot bath."

What he really wanted was to get these women, however be-
guiling, out of his hair so he could commandeer one of the tele-
phones nesting in every corner. With the musicians distracted, he
could phone for help.

Even then, of course, he would have to figure out whom
to call.

"Is there a bath?" Bridges asked, delivering the line perfectly
deadpan. "Or did the Shah share a toilet with the neighbors down
the hall?"

"There's no hall," Charlene said, taking Bridges seriously.
"There's no neighbors. This suite occupies the entire floor."

"I'm absolutely certain the unit has its own bath," Marlene said.
"I wouldn't be surprised if there were, in fact, two baths."

"Or even three," Charlene said.

"Let's check it out," Darlene said.

They laid down their instruments and exited through a set of double doors at the far end of the room.

Alone at last, Bridges took in the view. Somewhere beyond that parched landscape, he figured, past the sand, stubble, and scrub, lay sanity and salvation.

He heard the sound of water flowing—clearly, the musicians had located a bath. Bridges redirected his gaze from the desert to a suede recliner beside a low enamel table supporting a gaudy telephone, an acid-dream exaggeration of a clunky French antique. He walked over and sank into the chair, hefted the receiver, and began to dial, when a voice started speaking.

"Good evening. This is the operator. How may I direct your call?"

"My name's Bridges," he said. "Dwight Bridges, and–"

"I caught your late set Tuesday, Mr. Ritchie. You killed!"

"What?" Bridges said. "Oh." After a moment he added, "Thanks."

"My brother knows a busboy at the Silver Slipper whose postman delivers mail to a bellhop at the Sahara whose wife's best friend dates a pit boss related to a change girl at the Mint who scored a cancellation."

"That's great," Bridges said, nodding. "Can you connect me with the airport?"

"Airport?" the operator said. "You're looking to book passage to Hoggzswallow Hollow, West Virginia?"

"Why, yes, as a matter of fact. Any flight with connections through Charleston or Richmond will do. Since this appears to be Las Vegas, I suppose I'll have to change planes at O'Hare."

"When Jesus returns to Earth," the operator said, "even He will have to change planes at O'Hare."

The showgirls now suddenly reappeared, their breasts bobbing as they sprinted into the living room.

They fell upon Bridges.

"What's going on?" he asked them.

"Never mind what's going on," Darlene said. "Look what's coming off."

The women lifted his arms high. They yanked his tuxedo jacket up over his head as if it were a pullover sweater. "Bath time," Arlene chirped.

"You haven't a thing to worry about," the operator reassured Bridges, who continued holding the receiver to his ear.

Darlene bent down and unlaced his oxblood Ferragamos.

Marlene's fingers dropped to Bridge's belt buckle.

His body went rigid with resistance.

"What's with the shy stuff?" Marlene said.

She turned to her compatriots.

"Arlene? Charlene? Darleen? Turn away for a minute, will you? Mr. Ritchie is about to reveal his pink and wrinkled thingy."

Marlene giggled and made a grand show of averting her eyes.

"Your travel itinerary is all arranged," the telephone operator informed Bridges.

"It is?" he said, flailing for his southbound slacks.

"Mr. Scheib's taken care of everything," the operator said.

"He has?"

Charlene grabbed the phone from Bridges and crashed it back into its cradle.

He looked down to discover he wore only his shorts.

The musicians grabbed the elastic band, and in a flash the boxers swept past his toes.

In a futile attempt at modesty, his hands fell to his groin.

The women seized Bridges under his shoulders. They hauled him out of the chair. With balls bouncing, they propelled him through the door and down a corridor leading away from the living room.

The musicians dragged Bridges through sitting rooms, standing rooms, past a game room, media room, den, library, pantry, full-service commercial bar, full-service commercial kitchen, a single-lane bowling alley, and a single-lane indoor lap pool.

Though the suite contained no golf course, its immaculately trimmed putting green featured real Bermuda grass.

The party arrived finally at the Bedroom of Bedrooms, a master suite as huge as the hangar for the Goodyear Blimp.

The bed was roughly the size of Montana.

Billowing through a doorway to the bath wafted a cloud of steam.

The bath itself was no larger than ancient Rome's Baths of Caracalla. The walls, ceiling, and even the floor were mirrored. There was a professional shampoo sink as at a beauty parlor, and also a dressing table, a sit-down hair dryer, a shower grotto with multiple heads, and no mere tub but an immersion tank with displacement sufficient to float a Lexington-class aircraft carrier like the USS *Nimitz*.

Atop the water arose an Everest of pearlescent foam.

"You put in too much bath salts," Arlene reprimanded Darlene.

Bridges, however, who normally preferred a quick shower to wasting time in a tub, assured both of them that the bubbles were fine.

Lord in Heaven, Bridges thought, watching the lather rise. It struck him that these activities surely violated federal energy-conservation guidelines, which provided him with a sense of satisfaction.

All the same, he knew he should flee the joint, grab a cab, and head for the airport.

"Ready, girls?" Arlene sang out. "Heave!"

Bridges flew butt-first into the deep.

He surfaced spitting, sputtering, and wiping his eyes.

The water was too hot. To Bridges, this meant that it was just right. Not only was he pleased to be wasting energy, the scalding water also soothed and revived him. It reminded him that he was alive. Hadn't he extricated himself from the nightclub? Hadn't he ditched loathsome Buddy Scheib? Even if he wasn't yet back home in Hoggzswallow Hollow, settling in before the TV commercials with Mother, wasn't he entitled to a little rest and recreation?

The phalanx of parallel mirrors reflected a surreal view that stopped him cold: five-hundred exquisitely constructed young women, removing a thousand pasties, and kicking off an assortment of needle-sharp stilettos in numbers so vast as to impress even Imelda Marcos.

After a collective pause, the musicians shed their G-strings.

The mirrors now displayed a panorama of patchy, downy triangles, the vista calling to mind a sandy ocean floor replete with sea urchins and spiky saltwater anemones.

The women's motions appeared choreographed, like X-rated Rockettes.

In a hand-holding leap, the huddled, teeming masses—Arlene, Charlene, Darlene and Marlene reflected and re-reflected a trillionfold in the endlessly intersecting mirrors—joined Bridges in the tub. Their splash set off a tsunami, swamping Bridges, who coughed, gasped, and wheezed.

The sorry truth was that Dwight Bridges had precious little experience with naked women. There was that aberration in Cleveland at the Midwest Dealers Convention back in '70 or '68 or whenever. To be fair, he'd consumed no small quantity of spirits that night, and the woman turned out to be one among a sizable crew of professionals working the conference.

Though he didn't share the notion with other folk, for example his bandmates, it struck him that—what do they call it?—copulation was one vastly overappreciated enterprise.

As far as Bridges was concerned, if you wanted to know the whole truth and nothing but, the moment's euphoria all those years ago that Bridges had experienced in Cleveland hardly compared to a solid session in the crapper. After a dog, isn't man's best friend his hand? No risk of rejection or infection. No fees. No time-squandering flirting, courting, wooing.

He recalled an English literature class he'd been required to take during his two years at Monongahela Community College decades earlier. He couldn't remember if it was Keats or Yeats—he was certain it was one or the other—who asked: "Why does God build love's mansion in the place of excrement?"

At church, Pastor Pete disdained evolution and preached instead a principle he called Intelligent Design. Bridges could believe the Design part all right. It did not strike him, however, as the least bit Intelligent. Why would an all-knowing, all-powerful ruler of the universe require the spurting and squirting, the sweaty, stinky, clammy, gooey accouterments attendant to so existential a phenomenon as procreation?

Still, if only out of politeness, Bridges played along with his erstwhile quartet of companions.

"What this man needs, girls," Charlene announced to her colleagues, "is a little mouth-to-ding-dong resuscitation."

Bridges watched four heads vanish beneath the foam.

He thought he should rise to his feet and flee.

He rose, all right, but not to his feet.

Instead, he sank back in surrender, muttering silently to himself, What the hey.

CHAPTER
4

Bridges dropped off the lads back at Convy's Mobil and sprinted for home, to heck with fifty-five miles per hour. Then it occurred to him that scrutiny from law enforcement was something he should not encourage, most especially at this hour, and under these circumstances.

He slowed.

Alas, it was the slowing that caught the patrolman's attention, prompting him to pull Bridges over.

They came to a halt roadside, just across the highway from where the cable-laying crew had quit the day's dig. Orange trucks bearing the MidAtlantic Signal Corporation insignia were parked on the shoulder alongside gargantuan spools of coaxial. On this day alone, the crews had expanded the trench's reach nearly fifteen meters.

Soon enough, it would reach the central distribution hub south of Wheeling, connecting Hoggzswallow Hollow with the rest of the world.

"Everything all right, Dwight?" the officer inquired upon coming around to the driver's window.

"Absolutely, Al. Why in the world not?"

His feet shuffling on the floor between the brake and the accelerator, attempting to kick the paint canister out of view beneath the seat, Bridges reached into his pocket for his license and registration.

"You were driving so slow," Officer Alvin Henderson said, "it struck me there was some sort of trouble."

"There's trouble, all right," Bridges said. "This gas thing, this energy thing. I'm merely attempting to comply with recently issued federal conservation mandates regarding the operation of motor vehicles."

Goodness gracious, he thought, I'm talking like some kind of lawyer.

He handed his documents to Henderson. The officer accepted the papers without looking at them.

A sinking feeling settled over Bridges. Getting caught out late on the heels of the recent mischief was reckless in the extreme.

"There's talk of a new national speed limit, in case you don't know," Bridges told Henderson. He spoke the sentence with uncharacteristic sarcasm, which he immediately regretted.

"Naturally I'm familiar with speed limits, Dwight," Henderson explained patiently. "It's my professional responsibility. And it's my job, also, to inform you that driving too slow on a major thoroughfare can be every bit as hazardous as speeding."

"Trying to save gas is all."

"Quite the opposite. You want to find the point of maximal return relative to your octane usage."

Bridges resented the lecture. "Thanks so much, Al, for explaining that," he said, perfectly deadpan.

"What are you doing out at this hour? Band rehearsal run late?"

"Exactly right." Bridges nodded. "And just now I'm in a hurry to get home and catch my commercial."

"You know I have to write you up," Henderson said. "The law's the law; my hands are tied."

"I understand."

What Bridges understood was that, regarding law-enforcement issues, Hoggzswallow Hollow's Officer Alvin Henderson, while otherwise a decent enough fellow, was a by-the-books hardliner.

"I won't delay you any further," Henderson said, handing back Bridges's papers. "I'll drop off the ticket tomorrow."

"I appreciate it. Thanks, Al," Bridges said, for the first time in his life expressing gratitude to a cop for citing him for a moving violation.

Henderson got back into his car. In another moment the Ford Police Interceptor, a gussied-up Crown Victoria bearing front and rear push bumpers that weighed a ton each, executed a U-turn on Old Deerfield and drove away.

Bridges watched the vehicle vanish into the landscape. By Bridges's estimation, it did not appear to have exceeded fifty-five miles per hour.

He guided his LeSabre back onto the blacktop.

Soon enough, he pulled into his driveway.

He locked the car's doors, an unusual act in Hoggzswallow Hollow, where big-city precaution was considered unnecessary. He deposited the primer canister in the garage among a clutter of cans dating back to God knows when. Most of them contained house paint that had long ago congealed to concrete. He located a can of benzene and took it with him into the house.

"Dwight," a voice called out. "That you?"

Bridges was overcome by a peculiar urge to say No, it's Tricky Dick Nixon, it's King Fucking Farouk, it's the man in the motherfucking moon.

Instead, he called out, "Yes, Mother."

In the background played a Japanese sci-fi cheapie, dubbed into stilted English.

"Best hurry," Mrs. Bridges shouted. "Break's coming up any second."

Bridges made his way to the laundry sink on the service porch off the kitchen, slipped out of his shoes, and stripped off his ratty lambswool sweater. He seized a rag from a wicker basket and doused it with benzene.

He dabbed first at the shoes, then the shirt.

"Everything okay?" his mother said, shuffling in. "You're out mighty late tonight."

"Rehearsal ran long."

"Here, son," Henrietta Bridges said, reaching for his sweater. "Let me do that for you."

"No, no," Bridges said too quickly, yanking the garment away from her. "I've got it. I'll handle it."

"Don't be silly," she said, reaching again for the sweater.

"Damn it, Mother!" Bridges barked, snatching it back. "Didn't I say I'd take care of it?"

Lost in her granny gown, bathrobe, and an honest-to-goodness sleeping bonnet of a bygone era, Mother Bridges stood there, clearly wounded. "What's got into you?"

"This gas thing," Bridges said apologetically. "This energy crisis. It's got me all riled up."

"I understand."

"But that's no cause to snap at you, Mother. I sincerely apologize."

"Accepted."

Once again she reached for the sweater.

Once again Bridges grabbed it back.

"I told you I'd handle it!"

"What's happened?" Bridges's mother asked him. "What's so special about that sweater?"

"Nothing."

"What'd you get on it?"

"Nothing."

"Paint? Is that paint?"

"Are you all enjoying tonight's Fright Flick?" Wilbur Morton's ersatz deep-woods twang oozed from the TV. "We'll be getting right back to the movie after just a few words from some of the good folks who make it all possible."

"Here it comes, son," Mother Bridges said urgently. "You're gonna miss it."

"Dale's spot's first," Bridges told her. "Wilbur promised to run mine last. That's your best sales strategy, so he tells me. And he knows all about these matters. He's got—what do you call it?—media savvy. He told me so himself. Keep an eye on it for me, would you please? I'll catch up with you in a flash."

Henrietta Bridges waddled back to the living room.

Bridges finished his business on the service porch. The paint came off the shoes easily enough, but the sweater was stubborn. Bridges dabbed at the stain, pouring benzene onto it directly from the can. He bunched up the fabric and rubbed the cloth against itself, then washed it in the sink with soap and water.

All the while, he could hear the sound of the television. "Hi, everybody, and welcome to Dale Dixon's Datsun Depot. Are you ready for our Datsun Deal of the Day? It's a taupe 1200 Coupe Roadster Special."

He pronounced *taupe* as "tow-pay" and *coupe* as "coo-pay."

"Hurry, Dwight!"

"Coming, Mother."

Bridges continued working away at the sweater. Was all the paint gone? It was hard to tell. He rinsed it again, wrung it out, laid it over the drying rack.

"And finally, folks," Bridges heard Dixon declare in the background, "if you'll test-drive one of our fine-tuned, fuel-efficient vehicles, we'll give you, for free, one of our world renowned Dale Dixon Datsun Dish Diapers."

Bridges arrived at last in the living room, where Mother watched the TV from a sofa so decrepit that the Goodwill store would have rejected it. He settled his frame onto a padded Centreville rocker.

On the television, Dale Dixon whipped out an oversize kitchen towel that bore the legend *Dizzy Dale Dixon's Datsun Dish Diaper—Wipes Out the Competition*. "You can use it to clean your windshield," Dixon said, making extravagant sweeping motions in the air, "or you can put it to whatever suits your purpose."

In a flash, Dixon squatted low, sending his knees east and west as if dancing the Charleston. He whipped the cloth between his thighs and tugged it up to his crotch. Next, he rose upright and secured it at either hip with two oversized plastic safety pins that, even on black-and-white TV, looked pink. Now he jammed his thumb into his mouth, bugged out his eyes, wiggled his hips, wriggled his whole body, and clucked like a chicken.

Next to this clown, Bridges brooded, Jerry Lewis was as sober as Walter Cronkite.

He found himself staring at his own face.

"I'm Dwight Bridges of Bridges Buick on Old Deerfield in Hoggzswallow Hollow," he said, staring awkwardly into the lens, clad in his wrinkled cord pants, flannel shirt, and the ratty lambswool sweater that only moments earlier he had scrubbed in the utility-room sink.

"Everybody knows who you are, Dwight," his mother told him. "Everybody knows where the dealership is too."

"I'm sorry to interrupt your movie," he continued.

"It can't be effective salesmanship to open with an apology," Mother Bridges said.

"I have some pretty nice cars here at fair prices."

"Americans want more than nice cars at fair prices," Mother said. "You've got to spice things up just a touch, Dwight. You see the way Dale does it? That boy's got customers lined up and down the street."

"That boy sells cheap foreign product that runs a hundred miles on a teaspoon of fuel," Bridges said. "I'm no kind of carnival-sideshow barker. I'm a respectable businessman engaged in a respectable enterprise, trading respected and respectable American product. Dale traffics in shoddy merchandise manufactured by minimum-wage Asians, not solid American automotive stock but jerry-rigged kiddie cars."

"And what's so all-get-out respected and respectable about going bankrupt and starving?"

"Do these commercials really make a difference, Mother?" Bridges sighed. "With these damnable hills obstructing the signal, does anybody see them? There aren't but a half-dozen TV sets in all of Hoggzswallow Hollow. There's ours, Dale Dixon's, Wilbur Morton's, and just a handful of others. There's a single station with a three-watt transmitter, powered by a flashlight battery, broadcasting reruns of shows that were old even when they were new."

"Cable company's running a line in even as we speak. Gonna connect Hoggzswallow Hollow with the rest of the world," Mother Bridges explained patiently. "So it matters plenty. We're talking about attitude, Dwight. You can't stand up there, doing your impersonation of a wooden Indian, and hope to sell cars. Like it or not, salesmanship is show business. That's a plain and simple fact."

"What's a plain and simple fact is these gas lines," Bridges said. "I can't hope to move inventory with towel-headed sheiks holding back their oil, and the automobile market awash in foreign product, not to mention a certain foreign group exercising foreign influence over American foreign policy."

"Easier to criticize others than take a hard look into the dark night of one's own soul."

Bridges rolled his eyes as he always did when he recognized Mother plagiarizing five-and-dime metaphors from Pastor Pete's Sunday sermons.

He peered into the dark night of pixilated snow, fog, and static playing on the TV. Through the electronic murk, he beheld the image of two Japanese children toddling into a scientist's laboratory. In voiceover narration, a character proclaimed "…the solution to our problem is a little girl and boy," which Bridges's heard as "so-roo-shun to our prah-brem is a ridd-oo girh and baw."

The image now cut to a stop-motion animated vinyl lizard overturning a train whose locomotive bore the legend *Lionel*.

Bridges stood up, approached the TV, and reached for the switch.

"Leave it, Dwight," said Mother Bridges. "I'll just watch the littlest bit more of the movie, and then I'll turn in."

Bridges nodded and made his way to his bedroom.

There, he stripped off his clothes and donned his flannel pajamas.

He headed for the bathroom. He switched on the overhead bulb, stood before the toilet, peed, and flushed.

He moved over to the sink, washed his hands and brushed his teeth.

He pivoted and headed for the door.

He switched off the light, but it continued burning brightly.

CHAPTER
5

The glare was blinding.

The light crackled and spit. It sparked erratically, alternately dimming and brightening, calling to mind a carbon-arc movie projector with rods in need of realignment.

Bridges worried he had gone blind.

This was not the first time, however, he had experienced this phenomenon. If a fellow goes blind, he reasoned once again, he should see not whiteness but darkness.

As his vision cleared, he found himself standing in midday sunshine on the grounds of the Sa'dabad Palace, the chalk-white edifice constructed centuries earlier by the Qajar monarch. The walled, three-hundred-hectare complex was set in Shemiran, now a bedroom community of Greater Tehran.

Considering the unsettling nature of the circumstances, Bridges felt strangely calm.

Now he heard the sound of a helicopter.

A twin-rotor CH-47 Chinook, its body painted in desert camouflage, materialized in the sky above him. Bridges watched the hulking aircraft settle slowly onto the ground not far from where he stood, obliging him to turn his back to the flurry of pebbles and dust kicked up by the prop wash.

The engines quit, and the rotors ceased cranking.

From his location, Bridges could make out the windscreen fronting the Chinook's cockpit. He was close enough to observe the captain unbuckle his safety restraints and remove his over-sized headset.

He recognized the pilot as the fellow who, along with his entourage, had occupied the V.I.P. booth at the fabulous Starshine Dome of the phenomenal Desert Goliath Hotel, Country Club, Resort, Spa, and Casino in Las Vegas, Nevada.

A gate at the forward section of the Chinook rolled up. A segmented staircase unfolded, reaching for the pavement like an arm.

Shah Reza Pahlavi and his third wife, Farah, emerged from the craft. They made their way down the steps to the spot where Bridges stood.

"You killed!" said the Shah.

"I peed my pants!" said Queen Farah.

CHAPTER
6

B ridges awoke with a start to find himself alone in the tub.
From a distant corner of the penthouse, Arlene, Darlene,
Charlene, and Marlene could be heard gossiping as they packed
up their musical gear, their G-strings, stilettos, and tasseled pasties. Soon enough, they were gone from the suite.

At the tub's rim stood Buddy Scheib.

He held out a blue velour robe for Bridges that was so plush, so
generous with fabric, two people could have worn it at the same
time. Given the pale dawn creeping through the skylight, and the
piss-warm temperature of the bathwater, Bridges calculated several hours had passed since he and the women had surrendered to
saturated slumber. To Bridges, the wet, sloppy grindfest seemed
now but a vague recollection from the distant past of somebody
else's life.

He was too weary to resist as Scheib and a crack team of va-
lets shaved and combed him, then dressed him in Mack Weldon
underwear, a Van Heusen Lux sateen shirt, a three-piece tweed
ensemble from Brooks Brothers, plus hand-tooled loafers by
Bruno Magli.

He boarded the same limousine that, on the previous night,
had served briefly as the musicians' rolling recital hall. The vehicle
eased into motion. Not a minute later, it pulled up alongside a
private jet, no mere Lear or Gulfstream but a customized Boeing
777, its engines idling on the McCarran Airport tarmac strip reserved for noncommercial aircraft.

Bridges was settling into his recliner in the plane's oak-paneled
English-country-estate library when, with a lurch, the jetliner
came to life. It hesitated for a moment, amped up its engines, then
sprinted down the runway.

The craft was aloft when Buddy Scheib appeared at Bridges's
side and handed him two sheets of typed paper,

"Your speech," Scheib said.

"Speech?"

"For the Holocaust gig."

Bridges stared at him blankly.

"A little something the writers worked up," Scheib said, "not
that so monumental a talent as Richie Ritchie needs writers."

"Writers?"

"You don't have to follow it," Scheib reassured him. "Say what
you want, whatever comes to mind. Feel free to ad-lib. Do your 'A'
material, your late-set lounge act if it suits you. If you get lost, you
can cop to these pages."

"Pages?" Bridges said.

He stared at the document for a moment. He read aloud, "I
greet you this morning with vast pride but little pleasure."

He looked up at Scheib.

"What's this all about?" he asked. "Where are we going?"

"Come off it, Rich, will you?" Scheib said. "Where do you think we're going? Hoggzsfuckingwallow Hollow, West Fucking Virginia?"

Scheib laughed a little too heartily. He could see that Bridges was genuinely bewildered.

"Wow," Scheib said. "Them musician chicks really diddled your lobes, eh?"

He leaned in close and peered into Bridges's eyes. He wagged two fingers up and back, scant inches from his face. "How many fingers I got up, Rich?"

Bridges ignored the question and continued to study the pages.

"To be honored by a community so distinguished, so astute, so august," Bridges read aloud, "so dignified as those gathered here today, causes my heart to soar, my spirit to rejoice, even in surroundings so somber and sorrowful."

The plane's public-address system came to life. The pilot's voice flowed a touch too slowly, at a low pitch, as if from a tape recorder with weak batteries. "Please forgive me for troubling you, Mr. Ritchie," the Captain said, "but federal law requires that I ask you to extinguish all smoking materials, fasten your seatbelt, and make certain that your tray table and seatback are in the upright position as we prepare for landing."

Landing? Hadn't they taken off only minutes earlier? Hadn't they barely reached their cruising altitude? How could they already be approaching Charleston or Richmond or any other airport accessible to Hoggzswallow Hollow?

Bridges stuffed the pages into the pocket on the back of the seat before him, which contained an airsick bag and a laminated card bearing the standard protocols, including preparation for what was characterized as "a water landing." There was also a flexible vinyl placard reading OCCUPIED on one side and OCUPADO on the other.

The plane banked sharply, nearly hurling Buddy Scheib against the ceiling.

"Key-riced," Scheib said. "I'm returning to my seat and strapping down my balls. Seeya on terra firma." He vanished through a door into an antechamber several city blocks beyond Bridges's lounger. Through a porthole to his side, Bridges observed the rising sun, a phosphorescent tangerine disk the size of a Kennedy half-dollar, a thumbnail's breadth above the landscape behind him.

He recalled what he had learned eons ago while training for his Eagle Scout merit badge in Navigation.

At dawn, if the sun's behind you, you're traveling west.

Hoggzswallow Hollow, on the other hand, Bridges contemplated in despair, is due east.

CHAPTER
7

In the palace's vast Mirror Hall, which could have hosted a banquet seating hundreds, Bridges, the Shah, and Queen Farah feasted on kebabs, shawarma, tabbouleh, and fattoush.

He would have been happy for a Big Mac and fries at Hoggzswallow Hollow's lone McDonald's at Three Corners, the intersection of Deerfield, Old Deerfield, and New Old Deerfield or, for that matter, any of the planet's thirty-thousand Golden Arches outlets.

All the same, even if the grub was foreign, it was tasty.

Certainly it sated Bridges's considerable appetite.

Stationed discreetly behind the trio was a contingent of operatives, courtesy of SAVAK, the national Iranian organization overseeing security and intelligence.

"I'm so impressed," Bridges said "that you pilot your own helicopter. I can't imagine how you know what levers to pull, the switches, the knobs, the stick."

"I was trained in the army."

"It's only a little more complicated," Queen Farah said, "than operating an automobile, new or used, from Dwight Bridges Buick, of Hoggzswallow Hollow, West Virginia."

She and the Shah high-fived each other and shared a hearty laugh.

Not knowing what else to do, Bridges smiled and nodded and laughed a little too.

"Is there anything else you would like?" Farah asked.

"I'm stuffed," Bridges said.

"Excellent," the Shah said. "Come with me, and I'll show it to you."

Aides stepped forward.

In unison, they pulled back the diners' chairs.

The party rose to their feet.

Queen Farah took Bridges's hand, tenderly squeezed it, nodded, bowed, and departed through the chamber's main entrance, followed closely by her coterie of attendants.

Trailed by SAVAK operatives, Shah Pahlavi led Bridges away in the opposite direction.

They emerged from the White Palace and strolled over to the Green Palace.

The Shah led Bridges through the double front doors, which opened onto an ornately decorated foyer with two marble staircases leading up to a balcony above the entry.

It would have been the perfect spot for a rant from Mussolini.

Instead of climbing the stairs, Bridges was escorted to another set of steps at the atrium's far wall.

These stairs led only down.

Trailed by the bodyguards, Bridges and the Shah descended several flights. At the bottom, they trod along a dark corridor that ended at a steel door studded with wheels, locks, dials, and levers, like the entrance to a bank vault.

SAVAK personnel flicked a number of switches and spun some dials.

With a clanking of gears and a mechanical hum, the wheels started turning.

The door swung open.

Shah Pahlavi and Bridges entered a chamber the size of a racquetball court.

"Here it is," the Shah said.

Bridges regarded some sort of machine, not much larger than a Volkswagen Beetle, stationed at center. The device rested on a platform with built-in rotors, rollers, and wheels, clearly designed to enable it to position and reposition itself.

"It's the positron-emission muon ionic holographic tele-trans-porter," the Shah informed Bridges.

Bridges nodded.

"You must be eager to get home," the Shah said. "We'll set it for Hoggzswallow Hollow, West Virginia, eh? Two minutes is about one minute longer than the journey should take."

Shah Pahlavi stepped up to a control panel. He rotated a knob a quarter turn.

The apparatus started to vibrate.

The Shah attenuated some dials.

The pulsation intensified, evolving to a rattle. There was the sound of gears striving and failing to mesh, like that of a car—for example, a new or used Buick—that had thrown a connecting rod linking the piston to the reciprocating rotation of the crankshaft and its interlocking cams.

From the expression on the Shah's face, Bridges could tell that something had gone wrong. Clearly, the machine was not doing what it was designed to do. Whatever that might have been, Bridges hadn't a clue.

Now, atop the machine, a halogen-powered beacon came to life, twirling like the flasher on Officer Alvin Henderson's police-cruiser's roof.

A siren wailed.

"Damn!" said the Shah. "Mossad sent a team to fix this not two weeks ago. This is truly embarrassing."

"Not to worry," Bridges said.

"There's only one more of these devices in the entire world," the Shah said. "I'll have to take you there."

Bridges nodded slowly.

"Not to worry," he said again, clearly worried.

CHAPTER
8

A crowd was gathering around congregation B'Nai Ohev Shalom even at this early hour. But then, in Hoggzswallow Hollow, just two or three people constituted a crowd.

Melville Patterson, the arthritic janitor, not native to West Virginia but a refugee from New Jersey, scrubbed at the exterior walls and patio floor, struggling to eradicate the stain.

"Before you bust your butt with that steely wire brush and soapy water," Officer Alvin Henderson said, surveying the graffiti as he stepped from the Ford Interceptor, "let our forensics guys take some pictures for the file."

"Never mind pictures," Rabbi Solomon Geffner wheezed through the window of his vintage Packard as he pulled up to the scene. "Never mind forensics." His heavy black wool coat rising and falling with his labored breathing, he was out of the car even before it had come to a full stop. Notwithstanding the brisk November air, his brow glistened with sweat. "Never mind the file."

"It will serve as evidence, Sol," Henderson said, "in prosecuting the vandals who did this."

"Never mind vandals," the rabbi said. "Never mind prosecuting."

"Surely you want justice for your people and their temple."

"Justice is something our people have sought now for four thousand years. One day Mashiach will arrive on Earth, and then we'll know justice. I strongly doubt that will happen before, say, Arbor Day, whenever that is, or even a year from Purim."

"At least wait until the media have a chance to fulfill our task," Wilbur Morton called from behind the wheel of his own car as it pulled up to the shul.

"Media?" the rabbi asked. "Task?"

Morton piloted the decrepit Ford Fairlane wagon, which passed for the Channel 34 newsmobile, to a creaking halt beside Alvin Henderson's county-owned vehicle. The aged rattletrap bore the numerals 3 and 4 side by side on its doors in calligraphy almost as crude as the epithets defiling the temple.

"Alvin!" Wilbur Morton croaked. His voice was a marked contrast to the home-spun drawl familiar to his television audience. "Stand over there by the rabbi and be visual," he said. "Make like you're interviewing him. Pull out a pad, take notes, whatever."

Before the policeman could protest, Morton was dragging quartz lights, battery packs, tripods, cables, and an unwieldy Auricon sound-on-film 16mm camera from the station wagon's bed. "Give me a hand here," he said to nobody in particular, and nobody in particular came to his assistance.

Oblivious, Morton hopped around here and there, registering readings with a Weston reflective light meter. "Don't do anything till we're ready," he commanded janitor Melville, who stood by, leaning on his long-handled brush. "Nobody touch nothing till we roll."

"Keep on scrubbing," the rabbi instructed the janitor, counter-manding the newsman's order.

"But how will the nation know what happened here?" Henderson asked. "Don't you want to expose warped minds that perpetrate acts of hatred and bigotry? Isn't this America? Home of the brave, land of the free, and so on and so forth? Wasn't the American Revolution about putting an end to religious oppression? The last thing you want, Sol, is to cover this up."

"Respectfully, Al," Rabbi Geffner said, "to cover this up is not the last but the first thing I want."

Wilbur Morton looked up from the camera's open hatch and its chromium-plated sprocket wheels, where his stubby fingers strove to thread film. "Give that to us again in a minute, will you, Sol? Can you hang on for just one minute?"

"Another minute? Four thousand years Cossacks chase us ev-erywhere around the globe; we can wait another minute. We can wait another millennium, but that's not the point. The point is: Why make such a big deal out of this?"

"We're not making a big deal out of it," Henderson said. "The culprits, the racist hatemongers who committed this shameful, violent act, they are the people who make a big deal out of this."

"Shameful, yes," Geffner said. "But violent? Spray-painting slo-gans? It's adolescent hooliganism. It's mischief. It's delinquency. It's childish misbehavior. It's rowdy indecorum. But it's hardly vio-lence. The suffering of other oppressed groups, Negroes, for exam-ple, enslavement, lynching, arson, that's violence. What the Turks did to the Armenians early in the century, that's violence. If we wallow in outrage over slogans painted on a wall, if we marinate in vitriol over insults and slights, what's left for the Holocaust?"

Wilbur Morton succeeded in loading the film. He snapped shut the door on the side of the camera. He hefted the Auricon to his shoulder and commenced filming, wielding the lens like a garden hose, spraying the setting with footage. "Visual," he muttered under his breath as he photographed the graffiti.

"Wicked as this act may seem," the rabbi continued, "is it really anything more than a juvenile prank? Our faithful custodial engineer Melville here is a master of the janitorial arts. If we'll let him, he'll have all of this muck eliminated in an hour."

Behind them, the janitor resumed working away at the graffiti.

"Show this on the television?" Geffner asked. "Put pictures by the newspapers? You'll only provoke similar acts and actions and perpetrations by similar perpetrators. You'll inspire other fanatics to do likewise."

"Your point is well taken, Rabbi," Henderson said, "but it's not the American way. It's not the West Virginia way. It's not the Hoggzswallow Hollow way. Law-abiding, devout American citizens who assemble on consecrated ground for worship and prayer shouldn't have to worry about jackbooted thugs terrorizing their community."

Henderson paused for a moment to survey the graffiti.

"The desecration we see here," the police officer continued, "was committed by zealots seeking to obliterate our nation's tradition of ethnic toleration and religious freedom. Justice requires consequences."

"That's excellent," Wilbur Morton said, monitoring the proceedings through the camera's eyepiece. "Conflict, confrontation, controversy. Television at its best."

"Officer," the rabbi said, "the misconduct here was intended to garner precisely that kind of attention. Publicize this, and you'll have a rash of such incidents. Is that what you want?"

"Even if I agreed with you, Sol," Henderson told the rabbi, "I do not have the authority to enforce whatever laws I feel like enforcing. Like you, Rabbi, like all of us, I am bound by legal protocol and moral principle. Like you, I have a job to do."

"For thousands of years, Officer," Rabbi Geffner said, speaking now a little too patiently, as if addressing a child, "our people have dealt with much worse than youthful antics. Sophomoric horse-play should be the worst challenge we confront."

"Listen up, Officer," Wilbur Morton chimed in, his eye still stuck to the vinyl cup at the end of the lens. At the same time as he filmed the spray-painted epithets, he monitored the exchange between law enforcement and clergy. "We just happen to have a Constitution in this country," Morton said, "with that pesky First Amendment, which guarantees to the press certain inalienable freedoms, and the people's right to know."

"The people already know you, Wilbur," Henderson said. "They know what a lame and lamentable pinhead you are. They know you for the self-serving, boondocks-posturing, flyweight fool you just happen to be."

"You speak off the record?" Wilbur Morton said, the camera still cranking, its motor about as quiet as a cement mixer.

Henderson ignored the reporter's question and continued to address the rabbi. "It seems to me unacceptable, Sol, to permit the actions of a handful of mischief makers, probably just a bunch of dumb kids, to besmirch the identity of a whole community, a valley of overwhelmingly decent folk. The punks responsible for this hateful act have to be held accountable."

"A handful of mischief makers," the rabbi said, "in the beginning just a bunch of dumb kids, only a few years ago murdered six million of my brothers, sisters, parents, children, grandparents, aunts, uncles, and cousins. Featuring this on the news only inspires more bigots and bigotry."

In the background, a car pulled up. Both Baker brothers crawled out, unfolding their lanky frames like beach chairs.

Heaving an asthmatic sigh, the rabbi said, "Publicity is exactly what these hooligans seek. Reporting this in the newspapers and on the television merely plays into their hands."

He paused for another moment.

"Throughout our history we Jews eternally face this dilemma," the rabbi said. "Pretend and ignore, or confront and let the chips fly."

Rabbi Sol Geffner withdrew from his pocket a rumpled handkerchief about the size of a bedsheet.

"Don't get me wrong, Al," he said to the peace officer.

The rabbi mopped his brow.

He wadded up the hankie and stuffed it back into his pocket.

"Myself," he said, "most times, I'm a flying chipper."

CHAPTER
9

In Bridges's cabin, the light shifted radically.

The sun streaked up one wall, over cabinets crammed with leather-bound rare volumes, across the walnut-paneled ceiling, and down the far wall's ornate medieval tapestries with embroidered images of monks, maidens, and unicorns. Bridges's mind raced back to his Eagle Scout merit-badge training in navigation. The Pacific, smooth and glassy as a plate of Jell-O, previously dead ahead in the aircraft's flightpath, lay now at its tail.

The plane had reversed direction.

Bridges understood that he was now headed east.

If they had sufficient fuel, he calculated, if they flew far enough, they might even reach Hoggzswallow Hollow, West Virginia.

Instead, minutes later, they landed in Inglewood, California, the suburb to which Los Angeles assigns its international airport. Rather than approach a particular terminal, they taxied to undeveloped acreage at the east end of the field adjacent to a chain link fence crowned with concertina wire.

Beyond the barricade, there awaited a frenzied mob.

People brandished signs, flags, banners. There were also a squadron of press vehicles. In the saddles of CHP motorcycles sat gold-and-leather-clad officers so buff, so tanned, so blond, so blue-eyed, they could have been extras in a movie by Leni Riefenstahl.

Among the vehicles was also a burgundy stretch Caddy convertible with a bullet-proof Plexiglas bubble and garish mag wheels. It looked like the Popemobile pimped-up for Elvis Presley.

"Mr. Ritchie will have no statement," Buddy Scheib informed reporters as the entourage traveled the red-carpeted distance from the rollaway steps to the armored Caddy.

Suddenly, a fan bolted.

Bulling his way through the lines, he ran up to Bridges and thrust at him a pad and pen. A clutch of security guards promptly fell upon the intruder, knocking him to the pavement.

They slapped handcuffs on his wrists as tight as tourniquets.

"Stop!" Bridges shouted, surprising himself.

The scene fell instantly silent.

Bridges took a moment to recover his composure.

Then he said quietly, "Release him."

The guards looked to Buddy Scheib, who shook his head woefully up and back.

"I told you to let him go!" Bridges demanded with newfound zeal.

Again, the guards looked to Scheib.

Now, so did Bridges.

"It's dangerous, Rich," Scheib pleaded. "This is the left coast. There's every kind of weirdo. We can't take chances."

Bridges glared at Scheib.

Scheib waited one more moment, then nodded to the guards.

They released their captive.

The prostrate fan, middle-class, middle-aged, popped to his feet. "I only want an autograph. I'm waiting here since yesterday afternoon. I'm not complaining. To get this close to Richie Ritchie is my dream come true. Over the years," he said, "you've healed my heart. You've restored my soul. You've alleviated my sciatica. Forget the autograph. I'm really and truly sorry to have intruded."

Bridges bent down and lifted the fellow's pad from where it lay at the edge of the carpet. An arsenal of writing implements— felt-tipped, nylon, ball, Sharpie, fountain—materialized all around him, proffered by police, press, and publicists.

Bridges chose his weapon, a matte-black Montblanc Meisterstuck Classique that was as hefty as a flashlight.

He scrawled, "Best wishes."

He hesitated.

Now he hoisted the writing implement again above the pad. Slowly, deliberately, he wrote "Richie."

Again, he paused.

Then he added "Ritchie."

Bridges stared curiously at what he had written.

He returned the pad to the autograph seeker.

Overcome with emotion, the fan fainted dead away to the carpet.

CHAPTER
10

Officer Alvin Henderson was reluctant to park the Police Interceptor at its true destination, where anyone might see it. Instead, he pulled in behind a mini-mall hosting a florist, a pharmacy, and a bakery, all them closed for the night, a couple of blocks from where he actually intended to go.

People don't walk enough these days anyhow, he told himself. This energy thing, this whole damn energy thing, may God cut out my tongue for saying so, but if it discourages driving, if it motivates folks to get up off their duffs and walk, if it inspires souls to utilize long-neglected muscle fiber, it just might serve some useful purpose.

From the middle of the second block he could see there were no vehicles parked in front of Bridges's house.

He was disappointed.

Even as he knocked at the door, he knew knocking was useless. A house with nobody in it has a feeling about it. This was not just a precept of law enforcement; it was also plain common sense. When nobody's home, he had been taught at the academy, a house radiates a certain something, a hollow emptiness, an aura of vacancy.

He peered through the narrow glass panel on the wall beside the door. Though he expected it was futile to do so, he rapped on the glass and called quietly, "Dwight? You there? Mother Bridges? Anybody? Hello?"

He tucked Bridges's traffic ticket into the mail slot and then commenced a tour of the exterior.

The familiar LeSabre was there, sure enough, parked at the end of the driveway, partially visible behind the garage, a dilapidated standalone structure crammed with decades' worth of worthlessness. It struck Henderson as curious that Bridges's car was present but not Bridges. Stranger still, Henderson noted, when he approached the car and tried the doors, he found them to be locked. Folks in Hoggzswallow Hollow rarely locked their houses, let alone their cars.

He ran his hand over the hood.

It was warm to the touch.

Clearly, the car had recently been driven.

Officer Alvin Henderson walked up to the backdoor of the house, twisted the knob, and found that it too was locked. He removed a coiled steel cable from his pocket, a flexible jimmy maybe eighteen inches in length, which he carried for just such occasions—another aspect of his constabulary training.

Within seconds, he had the door open.

Inside, there was no hint of foul play, yet the policeman knew for certain that something was amiss. As the seconds mounted, the feeling grew more profound. He closed the door behind him and made his way to the foyer.

Now he heard the sound of a car pulling up, followed by doors opening and closing. Henderson peered through the window to the street, then stepped back into the kitchen.

Crouching low, he concealed himself between the refrigerator and range. The noises outside reminded him of sound effects from the golden age of radio, dramas like *Suspense*, or *Danger*, or *Lights Out*, the kind of programs they didn't have anymore, the kind of shows obliterated by the onslaught of television.

This struck Henderson as unfair.

Except for the one feeble UHF channel that nobody watched, Hoggzswallow Hollow had no television. From his hiding place in the kitchen, the officer could see in the adjoining room a floor-standing Crosley Corsair Concertone, the state-of-the-art in radio when Bridges's late dad had purchased it in 1948. The soap operas and serials the family used to enjoy had long ago been canceled. Besides news, weather, and top-forty pop, there was only a morning show produced for farmers, exploring issues like fertilizer and seed.

Henderson heard an anxious rapping at the door. "Dwight? You there? Dwight?"

Another voice muttered, "His car's here."

"Tell me something I don't know," the first voice barked. "Dwight? Mother B.?"

The knob rattled, and then the door itself creaked against the deadbolt. In another moment there was the sound of breaking glass, followed by the rasp of the deadbolt sliding.

For the first time in months, Officer Alvin Henderson withdrew the county's 9mm Smith & Wesson from its holster. Not moving, not breathing, he peered at shoulders and backs and legs passing by the kitchen and moving down the hall. One voice asked, "Where you think he would put it?"

Henderson quietly abandoned his position, stepping stealth-ily through the kitchen door, and moving down the hallway to the yard.

"There it is," one of the voices said, "just like I told you." This was followed by the squeak of faucets turning, and the rush of water filling a sink.

"Water won't likely do," the other voice said.

"Try benzene. You figure Mother B. keeps any benzene around the joint?"

"You figure she has detergent?"

"I ain't no washerwoman. Just grab it and let's get the hell out of here. We'll dump it somewhere is all."

Henderson replaced the gun in the holster and stepped into the utility room.

Both Bakers turned from the laundry sink and stared at him.

As did Ezra Convy.

Convy, Henderson said to himself. I completely missed Convy.

"What's it you want?" one Baker finally said.

The other said, "Badge don't give you no right to break and enter into people's houses, Al."

Ezra Convy said nothing.

"Somebody's broken and entered, all right," Henderson said. "You boys come by to do Dwight's laundry?"

The first Baker furtively slipped Bridges's paint-stained ratty lambswool sweater back into the sink. "Me and Ez and Warren, we been trying to reach Dwight is all, but he don't answer. We want to reschedule our band rehearsal is all, so we stop by is all."

"You break and enter, just to reschedule your band rehearsal?"

"What's it to you why we come over to Dwight's?" Warren said.

"Just a sweater's all it is, Al," Convy said. "Just Dwight's ratty lambswool sweater. So what?"

"So this," Officer Alvin Henderson said. "You're under arrest, the lot of you." He spoke the words coolly, matter-of-factly, as if commenting on the weather or the latest baseball scores.

"Don't make a fool out of yourself, Al," Curtis Baker told the policeman, as if he were offering useful advice that the officer would appreciate.

"You have the right to remain silent," Henderson said.

"Quit funning, Al. I mean it, too."

"In the event you choose to speak," Henderson continued, "any-thing you say can, and will, be used against you in a court of law."

Now there was the sound of feet padding their way down the hallway.

Henderson went silent, and the intruders stiffened.

The police officer's hand once again went to his holster.

Mother Bridges entered.

She wore her granny gown, bathrobe, and sleeping bonnet.

In her arms she cradled a Remington Model 870 Express Super Magnum hardwood pump-action shotgun.

CHAPTER
II

Bridges was so weary that he slept through several takeoffs and landings required for refueling.

Their final destination lay a couple of thousand miles beyond Teheran. The Shah had told Bridges that under normal circumstances they would have traveled by jet since, even with a decent tailwind, the Chinook's range was only three-hundred nautical miles.

Of course, the Pahlavi regime had a substantial fleet of sophisticated aircraft, gifts over the decades from Truman, Eisenhower, Kennedy, Johnson, and Nixon. Whatever disagreements existed among the various presidents regarding polices domestic and foreign, all deemed it essential to send tons of costly war gear to the Shah.

If America failed to do that, the Soviets would seize Iran and turn it into yet another Turkestan, Uzbekistan, Tajikistan, Kyrgystan, or some other Stan.

Soon after that, the commies would storm the American border at El Paso.

The equipment ranged from a just-for-fun two-seater Icon A5 Amphibious Light Sport Model MDX, to the Lockheed Martin F-22 Raptor and the General Dynamics F-16 Fighting Falcon, to the still-experimental Airbus A300B. The Airbus was large enough all by itself to deliver the entire population of a town the size of, say, Canton, Ohio, to wherever it wanted to go. The Wright Brothers' flight at Kitty Hawk could have been made entirely inside its main cabin.

During his training at the US Air Force Academy in Colorado Springs, the Shah, an aviation enthusiast since boyhood, had acquired the ability to pilot every one of those planes.

Nevertheless, for travel to the armed services airfield outside Qa'en in South Khorasan Province, to prep whatever alternative airship they had selected, not to mention the bureaucratic and logistical protocols required for such a changeover, would have them at their destination at the same time as the Chinook, which was primed and poised for flight at this very moment, mere steps from where they stood.

More to the point, however, as the Shah told Bridges, he really loved helicopters. "You don't need any airport," he explained, as if Bridges didn't know that. "You want to set it down somewhere, you set it down somewhere."

"Anywhere," Bridges said, nodding.

"Right," said the Shah, also nodding.

They boarded the very same Chinook that had delivered them to their present location.

Even landing and taking off to refuel—at Hamedan, Ramadi, Rutba, and Al Qurayaat—they arrived at their destination just past sunset, with the sky still bright enough to read the *New York Times* or the *Times of London* or any other *Times*.

As the Shah set the chopper down on an airfield at the edge of the Sinai, not twenty-miles from the top-secret underground installation at Waadi Rum, Bridges was just coming around from his nap.

It was only a couple of hours drive to Tel Aviv.

CHAPTER
12

The Caddy was in motion even before the doors slammed shut. Bridges was just now beginning to savor the tumult and attention surrounding him, even if only a little.

With police vehicles leading and trailing, their blood-orange/ ice-blue emergency lights whirling, Bridges cruised down a street adjacent to the airport whose sidewalks were jammed eight-deep with cheering fans. The mobs pressed against barricades before the topless bars, bottomless bars, massage parlors, porn shops, and sex-toy emporia common both to the era and the area, lining the boulevards with vast billboards bearing slogans in Japanese, Arabic, Korean, Tagalog, and in some instances even English.

One read *Live Nude Girls!*

A competing establishment across the boulevard boasted *Nude Live Girls!*

Yet another: *Girls! Nude! Live!*

And another: *Live! Girls! Nude!*

The cars squealed around corners: Spitfire Way, Hellcat Lane, Airfoil This, Airdrome That, and street after street labeled in Spanish: La Something This, La Something That, La Something Else.

They drifted through what passes for winter in Los Angeles. The temperature was in the mid-sixties, which to locals was bracing. Airbrushed, time-lapse, chrome-plated, Day-Glo clouds drifted across the sky as if matted in by Technicolor film-lab specialists on acid.

The motorcade zigged through convoluted intersections, then zagged onto an actual freeway.

Freeway, so this is your freeway, Bridges thought, as traffic parted before them like the Red Sea for Moses. They drifted among the lanes, any one of which all by itself was as wide as Old Deerfield in both directions.

What impressed Bridges most of all, however, were the buttons.

Vinyl disks embedded in the pavement, protruding a quarter inch above the roadbed, articulated each lane. Changing lanes, which required driving across the buttons, produced a ratchet effect, a buzz. In a town notorious for drivers changing lanes just to change lanes, Bridges appreciated that the buttons were a safety feature designed to alert motorists, should their vehicle stray from the right of way. At the same time, they imbued the driving experience with texture and tactility, the palpability emblematic of Southern California car culture.

Off to Bridges's left—that'd be north, he calculated, once again calling upon his Eagle Scout training—weren't mere foothills but honest-to-God snowcapped mountains; they were so picturesque, they could have been painted by Disney background artists.

This is Los Angeles? wondered Bridges. Where's the plastic? Where's the smog?

In the distance, ahead of the caravan, lay an actual skyline.

Skyline?

The city was a formless blob of suburbs, Bridges had heard, one bleeding into the next. He hadn't read Gertrude Stein, so he would not know that she had said of LA, "There is no there, there." Still, here was a downtown as cocky and self-assured as any known to Dwight Bridges: sleek high-rises of glass, stone, and steel, asserting an identity leavened by tons of attitude.

Soon enough, those buildings passed overhead as the motorcade, a disjointed mechanical serpent, slithered through a concrete canyon, a slot ten lanes wide and two stories below street level. Now the convoy veered vaguely north, then northwest, heading for the cluster of dusty blond hills called Hollywood.

CHAPTER
13

"You have the right to an attorney," Alvin Henderson said, handcuffing Ezra Convy to one of the Baker brothers, and the other Baker to himself. "In the event you cannot afford an attorney, the court will appoint—"

"I can afford twenty damned attorneys, Al," said Convy, cutting him off, "and I just may hire that many in order to sue your sorry ass for false arrest and felonious stupidity." He turned now to Mother Bridges and said, "Please pardon my language, Henrietta."

Mother Bridges nodded politely to Convy. Her Remington Model 870 Express Super Magnum hardwood pump-action shotgun resided where she had set it, upright on the floor, leaning against the Crosley radio.

Henderson led the men out of the house.

In the evening air, the Bakers looked to Ezra Convy as their spokesman.

"See here, Al," Convy said, the tone of his voice now concilia-
tory. "Let me explain, okay?" He hoped against hope that nobody
would observe this curious entourage, shackles clanking, as its
members trudged along the sidewalk fronting Bridges's house.

Except for Henderson and the detainees, the street was deserted, which was not at all unusual in Hoggzswallow Hollow at this
or virtually any other hour. "We were trying to get hold of Dwight
is all. We were concerned about Dwight."

"Where is he? Where's Dwight?" Henderson inquired as if
merely curious, shifting the Buick dealer's ratty lambswool sweater
to his shackled hand.

"That's what we wanted to know. Don't you see? Like I already
told you, Al, that's what we were trying to find out."

"So without knocking, without nothing, you just smash a window and invite yourselves in."

"We wanted to notify him that we rescheduled our band rehearsal. We couldn't reach him by phone, not here at his house, not
by his dealership, not by nowhere." Convy strove to maintain the
chat's congenial cadence. "We feared for his safety."

"In order to reschedule your band rehearsal," the lawman said,
"you break into Dwight's house and do some laundry?"

He shifted the sweater to his free hand and held it scant inches
in front of Convy's face.

"What do I want with that?" Convy said, as if viewing the
sweater for the first time. "I don't want nothing with that." He
grimaced and wrinkled his nose.

"Let's go, boys," Henderson said, steering the team toward the
county's car.

"You can't be serious, Al," Convy said. "You're not taking us in."

"Taking you and booking you. Got to do it, don't I?"

"No, you don't, Alvin. You'll just make a fool of yourself, I
guarantee it."

"That's my own worry, don't you think?"

"Look, Al, listen and look." Convy's inflection now betrayed a sense of dread.

This guy is sincerely reluctant to accompany me to the station, Henderson realized. Naturally, under such circumstances, any-body'd be reluctant. Aren't they always reluctant? Over the de-cades, he had never encountered a perp who was eager to take a ride downtown.

Still, Henderson noted, this old boy's singularly stressed.

"Listen and look," Convy said. "Me and these here Bakers, we three of us get that you're doing your job. We three of us always support your police forces, your law and order, all that. Everybody knows that. You'd be making a terrible mistake bring-ing us in. Even though we're innocent of any wrongdoing, we're also eager to avoid any spectacle, not to mention unnecessary expense to the township, the county, the state, the nation, what-ever, wherever, whoever."

"Let's go, fellows."

"Listen up, Al. What say you just forget all this, and we go our separate ways? Nobody would know. And in consideration for your good sense, why, we'd make it worth your while in some manner you'd be sure to appreciate."

"Get in the car," Henderson said.

"How's two hundred?"

This is serious stuff, the police officer reckoned. More so than I imagined.

"Okay, three hundred. Talking cash money. What do you take home in a month? Couldn't you use three hundred cool, crisp, American greenbacks?"

From Henderson, silence.

"All right, all right. Five hundred, you listening? Five hundred, plus I pump you all the goddamn gasoline you goddamn need."

"Al rips off his fuel from the county anyhow," the younger Baker grumbled.

"Shuttup your mouth," Convy snapped.

He turned back to face the officer. "So, Al? What do you say? Do we have a deal?"

CHAPTER
14

The endless motorcade, the Richie Ritchie rolling light show, arrived at last in Elysian Heights, a ramshackle neighborhood east of Hollywood metastasizing out of downtown Los Angeles like a tumor. The automotive regatta pulled to a stop before the former Mack Sennett Studio, a bygone silent-movie lot that had been retrofitted for television.

Bridges smiled and nodded, nodded and smiled at the technicians, office personnel, grips, carpenters, plumbers, electricians, hairdressers, wardrobe and makeup artists, all of them gaping in awe as he and his entourage sailed past. They arrived finally at a soundstage, where whatever was scheduled to happen would happen.

The brooding cavern featured bleachers packed with spectators, rising all the way to the light beds.

Up front, carpeted risers supported six leather-and-chrome chairs.

All but one were occupied.

At center sat a man wearing a gray suit, a gray smile, and a mane as silver as the chairs' chromium frames. Here was a fellow born to media punditry, exuding an air of authority and respect, at once casual and contemplative, Hugh Downs on steroids. He resolutely shouldered the gravitas associated with early '50s Sunday-morning culture-vulture programming, shows like *Open End* and *Omnibus*, intellectual fare hosted by highbrow moderators like Edward R. Murrow, David Susskind, and Alistair Cooke.

Even if Bridges had no clue as to the emcee's identity, he recognized the members of the panel easily enough: Jerry Lewis, Mel Brooks, Don Rickles, and Milton Berle.

Catching sight of Bridges, the comedians rose in unison.

As if their moves had been choreographed, they pivoted a hundred-eighty degrees so that Bridges was now looking at their backs. En masse, with Bridges and his entourage and the entire studio audience looking on, they unbuckled their belts.

They dropped their trousers, exposing their underwear.

They bent forward.

In one collective moon, they tugged down their drawers, flashing for Bridges their bare butts.

There was a screaming, cat-calling chorus of hoots and hollers and grunts and gasps and laughter from the technicians and audience and legions of behind-the-scenes hangers-on, as if there were a competition to determine who could howl the loudest.

The panel members themselves now broke rank, stamping mightily upon the ground, foaming at the mouth in bogus hilarity, as they restored their trousers to the upright position.

In what was clearly a well-practiced gesture, the moderator covered his eyes and tittered good-naturedly through the splayed fingers of his right hand. His demeanor proclaimed that here sat a public intellectual, an arts maven, a critic, a gentleman, a scholar, but not anybody too cultivated to enjoy a lusty righteous chuckle.

After what felt like a half hour, the comedians buckled their belts, turned, and surrounded Bridges, glad-handing him, back-slapping him, applying sloppy kisses to both cheeks and full on the lips, all the while murmuring Boychik, Bubby, Beauty, Cutey, Sweetie, Dah-link.

Grunting like a ram in heat, Don Rickles jammed his tongue deep down Bridges's throat, clear through to his epiglottis.

At last, a cordon of studio pages came to the rescue, extricating Bridges from the knot of jokesters.

They settled him into a chair at the panel's center.

The comedians retreated to their stations.

Technicians affixed lavaliere microphones to their lapels.

"We're going to start rolling in just several seconds, gentlemen," said the floor manager, standing midst a tangle of cable. He wore a telephone-operator's headset with a mouthpiece that bobbed an inch in front of his lips.

He waited patiently.

Now an indistinct voice crackled in his earphones.

The floor manager alerted the assembly: "Ready to roll!"

"I don't know about you guys," Don Rickles said, "but I been rolling since Thursday."

"I been rolling since April," Mel Brooks said.

"I been rolling since Simchat Torah," Milton Berle said.

The moderator smiled at Bridges. "We're grateful you could join us," he said. "You look wonderful."

"Hey, thanks," Jerry Lewis said, as if it were he who was being addressed. "I feel good, though I have a rash on my scrotum." His knees fell apart. He plunged both hands inside his pants and scratched vigorously at his crotch.

"You still believe that's just a cold sore?" Milton Berle asked him.

Lewis let out not a raspberry, not a moist, buzzing Bronx cheer but a sound way back in his throat intended to mimic an unsuccessfully suppressed fart. It came across as a French horn in the lower register, as if escaping between his buttocks slowly, but not slowly enough. "Oh, excuse me," he said, and promptly let rip another.

"No he don't," Rickles said. "He don't look wonderful. He looks like hell. He looks sick. He looks disgusting. He looks like he just now tumbled out of a whorehouse staffed by Latvian midgets." He reached over and took Bridges's face in his hands. "Richie, you all right?" He turned to the bleachers. "Medic! Stretcher! Anybody here know CPR?"

"Know her?" Mel Brooks said. "I dated her."

"CPR?" asked Milton Berle. "I'm not sure. Can you hum a few bars?"

"Hum a few bars?" Rickles said. "You can't even walk past a few bars without stopping in to get pickled."

"Ten, nine, eight …," the floor manager counted.

"Get this guy," Rickles said. "Will you get this guy? He's counting! Oh, Mommy, Mommy! I'm counting!"

"Seven, six, five …"

"What is this," Rickles continued, "Cape Fucking Canaveral? When's the rocket go up, buddy? Didn't anybody tell this puttz you start with *one* and go forward? He was absent from school the day they taught that? Where do they get the crew around this joint? From the Albanian Merchants Association?"

"You can't get decent help these days," Milton Berle said.

"Tell me about it," Mel Brooks said. "Try to get somebody who does windows, just try. Does this guy do windows?"

Lewis let loose another simulated fart, and now a real one. "Oh, excuse me," he said.

An apologetic expression took hold of his face.

He let loose another.

A red light came aglow atop the center camera. The floor manager pointed at the moderator, who peered solemnly into the lens. "I'm Chet Champion," he said. "Welcome to People Television's unique series of seminars evaluating, examining, and exploring *Our American Arts*. Today we focus upon comedy. To help us, we have some highly credentialed experts who'll comment on the nuts-and-bolts of contemporary American humor."

"I don't know from bolts," Mel Brooks said, scanning the panel, "but it looks to me like you got here plenty of nuts."

"Let me introduce our panel."

"Who's stopping you?" Rickles said. "What's with this schlub?" He turned to Milton Berle. "Who's he talking to?"

"He's talking to your mother," Jerry Lewis said.

"Hey," Milton Berle said. "Let's leave mothers outta this."

"Don't worry," Lewis responded. "Your mother's been out of it for years."

"Yeah, Miltie," Rickles agreed. "From around the time you were born."

"Listena this guy," Berle said. "A walking argument for compulsory sterilization. And he raps my mother."

Slogging through the blizzard of abuse, Champion eventually managed to corral the conversation enough to introduce the panel. The wisecracking and frantic energy subsided. In short order, there unfolded a facsimile of weighty intellectual discourse.

"Your cinematic arts is a special enterprise," Jerry Lewis said, now donning his "serious" mask. "Three decades and fifty-five pictures have taught me something about that."

"Tell us," Champion said, "about the unique challenges confronting filmic comedy." He sat back in his chair, scrutinizing panel member Jerry Lewis as if he were Albert Einstein on the brink of divulging relativity.

Bridges surveyed the collection of comic luminaries. He took comfort in the shelter of his anonymity. He would simply listen to the conversation and, soon enough, wake up to find himself safe and secure at his Buick dealership in Hoggzswallow Hollow, West Virginia.

"Your juxtaposition of images," Lewis said, "one after the next, this sets up special characteristics which I in my own cinema encounter in the composing of my own films, as it were. For example, it raises right away questions so basic to comedy in general. Like your timing, your whole rhythm, so to speak, your whole tone, per se, which is essential insofar as comedy is concerned and involved."

Bridges scanned the faces of the panel. Zany, wacky wisecrackery had given way to profundity and solemnity. Never in history, Bridges imagined, had there been so earnest an ensemble, so intense a deliberation. Next to these guys, Roosevelt, Churchill, and Stalin at Yalta were the Three Stooges.

"Mel Brooks," Champion said, "regarding the comedic genre, you're an acclaimed genius. Perhaps you could shed some light on this issue."

"Before I shed some light," Brooks said, "maybe I should light some shed, otherwise nobody will be able to see, since it's so dark in there, in the shed, get it?"

The audience and panel sat there in silence.

Brooks pivoted now toward sobriety. "Comedy, see," he said, "is a man's soul. You know what I'm talking?"

The panel members nodded in agreement. Clearly, they knew what he was talking.

Chet Champion, along with all the others except for Bridges, also nodded.

"It's like, you take all the madness in the world," Brooks continued, "you turn it around, you know, and you give it your own perspective, your own perceptions." He turned to his fellow panelists. "You fellows know what I'm talking?" The panel members stepped up the pace of their nodding.

"I know exactly what you're talking," Don Rickles volunteered. "You show something in a new light. And then you got comedy."

"Exactly," Lewis agreed, joining the nodding competition.

"You show the people," Milton Berle said, "something in some way they, the people, they haven't seen it yet in that way, that particular way, till before you just now showed it to them, and what you get in that case is comedy. You fellows concur?"

Murmuring assent, rocking back and forth in their chairs like Haredi davening in shul, it was clear that the fellows concurred.

Even Chet Champion concurred, and he wasn't really one of the "fellows."

Bridges alone did not concur, but then neither did he not concur. He merely sat there, blissfully ignored.

"Consider for a moment," Don Rickles said, "this whole broad concept of timing. Timing, just timing, is one whole broad concept, one whole broad aspect to consider. When I'm working a room, Vegas, wherever, say I'm working a room, and—"

"Hold it, Don," Milton Berle said. "Chet, fellows, I think we ought to explain to the people what it is we mean by these technical terms. The whole technical jargon of the craft, see. Like, for instance, Don here mentions timing. It's all well and good for us professionals who understand the business, the art, the craft, but we shouldn't make assumptions about the viewing audience. We owe it to them to define our terms, to define our definitions."

Berle now turned to look directly into the camera.

"Timing," he continued, "see, that's the cadence you build up, your flow, how you punch your routine, your sketch, your skit, your turn, your act, your routine, your number, your whatever." He paused to let his words sink in. "You get what we call a rhythm building, see, a flow, then you punch it and you're on your way. The fellows understand," he said.

Indeed, judging from the expressions on their faces, and the way their bodies swayed and shifted in their chairs, it was clear that the fellows understood.

"Exactly right," Jerry Lewis said. "Take, for example, my cinematic motion picture film cinema comedy *The Nutty Professor*."

"Take it, please, somebody! Anybody!" said Mel Brooks.

"Hey, Mel, come on now, let's cool the clowning if it's possible, just for a minute, okay? What do you say?"

"Absolutely," Brooks said. "Sorry, Jer."

"I mean the audience, here in the studio and at home watching on their television sets—"

"I hope to Christ they ain't watching on their toasters," Rickles said. "I hope they're not watching on their vacuum cleaners."

"That's exactly what I'm talking about," Lewis said.

"I know what Jer's talking about," Brooks said. Turning to Rickles, he said, "Don, I know what he's talking about."

"Okay, okay," Rickles said. He trotted out some silly faces, then smiled meekly.

"I happen to view the audience as the central entity in the performance process," Jerry Lewis said. "It's to them, God willing, we turn, and with His good grace, we attempt to reach their humanity. Now, in my movie which I made, *The Nutty Professor*, which Charlie Chaplin himself personally, by the way, told me personally, Chaplin did, is the greatest movie ever made by anybody—not just comedy but in any category—I'm just telling you what Chaplin personally told me himself personally. In *The Nutty Professor*, I do a sketch where my camera trucks forward as my main character emerges from my university campus. I was utilizing my 35-millimeter NC Fries Reflex Image Capture Mitchell, incidentally—that's my special motion-picture camera which the Mitchell people especially designed for me at my request, and they adapted it for me to my specific specifications. I'm shooting with my two-inch, and my gaffer's keeping down my lumens as I've instructed him, because I'm working for this subtle, intimate effect, see."

Lewis stood up and began pacing back and forth before the panelists as if to demonstrate this subtle, intimate effect.

"My character, the professor, he's sedate and sophisticated, Mr. Joe Knowledge, like they say."

Lewis assumed an arthritic posture.

An affectless trance took hold of his countenance.

"Okay," Jerry Lewis said, "now, suddenly, the guy changes, he becomes this totally different character, who I call 'The Idiot.'"

Lewis morphed into The Idiot, whose bearing and movements called to mind a patient with a degenerative neurological disorder. Hijacked by seizures, spasms, and tics, his body twitched and writhed. He hobbled up and back the length of the panel.

The live studio audience couldn't figure whether to laugh or cry, so they chortled.

"You folks get the idea," Jerry Lewis said.

"You folks get the idea," moderator Chet Champion said.

"Flaboydle, boydle, blab, blah, blah-boydle," Lewis said, spittle foaming at his lips and dribbling down his chin. "Hella-haven," he continued. "Flydle, flaboydle."

The titter among the audience swelled to a chuckle.

"You folks get the idea," Chet Champion said again.

"Flaboydle, boydle, blaboydle," Lewis said. "Hella-haven."

At last he stopped.

Once again, he donned his Serious Artist persona.

"Anyhow, you get the idea," Jerry Lewis said.

"You folks get the idea," Champion said yet again.

Now resuming his Human Being, Jerry Lewis reclaimed his seat. Champion started to applaud, and in a moment the audience joined him, dutifully providing an ovation.

"Marvelous, Jer," Milton Berle said.

"Erwin Panofsky," Champion said, "in his monograph *Meaning in the Visual Arts*, discusses the dynamization of space, on one hand, and the spatialization of time, on the other. Mel? Don? Milton?" He turned to Bridges. "Richie? Have you run into these twin concepts with regard to practicing the comedic arts?"

"I have," Milton Berle readily affirmed. "I certainly have."

"I haven't," Don Rickles said.

"I've run into one of them but not the other," Mel Brooks said.

"I've run into the other," Jerry Lewis said. "Whichever one Mel didn't run into."

Bridges said nothing.

"Come to think of it," Rickles reconsidered, "though I haven't run into them, I've jogged into one or the other. Jogged," he said again.

"Richie Ritchie," Champion said. "Do you yourself plan someday to approach comedy from the standpoint of cinema? You've enjoyed vast success in nightclubs and now television, which, it might be suggested, is film delivered via an electronic platform, don't you agree?"

"What?" Bridges said, after he realized that Champion was addressing him.

"I think I can paraphrase," Rickles jumped in, rearranging himself in his chair and tugging at a pair of invisible suspenders. "Get ready, Rich. You ready? Okay, here goes. What with the spatialization of your pimples, and considering also the blah, blah, blah, the dynamization of your mother, does it ever occur to you to investigate the perimeter of your parameters, or the strictures of your structures, those optical aspects, the visuality of this medium, or that medium, or another medium to be named at a later date?"

"I thought we're leaving mothers out of this," Jerry Lewis said.

"Medium rare," Milton Berle said. Now he said, "On second thought, I'll have the fish."

"But seriously," Champion continued through spasms of laughter that resembled epileptic convulsions, "Richie Ritchie, what's your reaction to the prospect in your future of a venture in motion-picture comedy?"

"I enjoy a good motion picture comedy," Bridges said.

"Did you like my latest," Mel Brooks asked, "*The Twelve Chairs*?"

"*The Twelve Chairs*, did you say?" Bridges asked. "That's a movie?"

"No," Brooks said. "It's a freaking pastrami sandwich. You didn't see it? It's okay, Rich, I forgive you. Nobody saw it. My mother didn't see it."

"I thought we're leaving mothers out of this," Don Rickles said.

"I saw part of it," Milton said. "I walked out after five chairs."

"With an ass as fat as yours," Mel Brooks said to Milton Berle, "you need five chairs just to sit down."

"If we could return to the subject for a moment, gentlemen," Chet Champion said, turning to Bridges. "Richie Ritchie, are you tempted to engage a venture into film?"

"I like a good film," Bridges said.

"This is terrific, this is terrific. I gotta take notes on this," Rickles said, pulling a phantom notepad from the air and grasping a virtual pencil. He waved his hand in an exaggerated scribbling motion. "He. Likes. A. Good. Film," Rickles scrawled in the ether.

Champion and the panelists all stared at Bridges.

"As far as my making a movie, I don't know. What do I know about movies?" Bridges asked.

"If Chet knew," Rickles said, "would he ask?"

"I don't know much about moviemaking. Come to think of it, I don't know anything at all about making movies. Even home movies. I don't have a camera."

"He. Likes. A. Good. Movie," Rickles wrote once again in the air.

"Truth to tell," Bridges continued, "this whole thing, this Richie Ritchie business, it's all a mystery to me."

"Uh-oh," Jerry Lewis said. "This ain't no set. This ain't the Comedy Store. This ain't the Laugh Factory. This ain't no guest shot on Johnny Carson. We're not supposed to cop to our standup routines here."

"There's no stopping him," Mel Brooks said. "Here it comes."

"Watch out now," Milton Berle said.

The audience simmered in anticipation.

"See," Bridges pleaded. "I'm no comedian. I really mean it. Honest. My true name is Dwight Bridges." The audience was laughing out loud now, their shoulders heaving. "I've said it before, I'll say it again: I'm a car dealer, Buicks, new and used, from–"

"Hoggzswallow Hollow, West Virginia!" the audience and panelists and moderator, even the technicians, the cameramen, the floor manager, all howled.

The audience rose to its feet, hooting its approval.

The panelists arose from their chairs.

Bridges remained seated.

Moderator Chet Champion, and panel members Milton Berle, Jerry Lewis, Mel Brooks, and Don Rickles, formed a semicircle behind Bridges, their hands clapping and jaws grinning in worshipful tribute.

CHAPTER
15

The Chinook settled nowhere near Tel Aviv but instead onto the sands of the Sinai Desert hundreds of miles away, just outside the entrance to a top-secret underground Israeli military base. The installation had been dug out of the earth forty miles north of the Suez Canal, not far from the recently occupied Egyptian village of Kadesh Barnea.

Israel, upon being attacked by its neighbors for the fourth time in its quarter-century history, had seized the entire Sinai Peninsula right up to the Egyptian border, an area by itself larger than all of Israel. From sandbagged emplacements on the northern rim of Suez, even without field glasses you could make out the monoliths at Giza.

A dark joke of the era: Come to Israel, see the pyramids.

Bridges and Shah Pahlavi emerged from the chopper to be greeted by an armed escort assembled for their security. They were

ushered to a pair of seats in the rear of an olive-drab armored
Jeep. With command vehicles fore and aft, they were driven to the
mouth of a tunnel leading into the underbelly of Jebel Musa, a
mountain rising seven thousand feet above the landscape.

The procession snaked its way along a narrow roadway running
beneath the parched terrain.

After a mile or more, the entourage emerged into a vast
subterranean facility carved out of bedrock. There were posted
guards, modest sleeping barracks for crews maintaining the installation, a cafeteria, a commissary, and even half a soccer field
for the staff's recreation.

There was also a hi-tech scientific laboratory.

The procession came to a halt.

Uniformed commandos led Bridges and the Shah into the lab.

They were greeted by two scientists.

Chaim Yitzkowitz, a theoretical mathematician, short and
stocky like a fireplug, was in his mid-twenties. Like most Israelis,
his religious identity was for the most part secular. Nevertheless,
he wore the kind of unruly beard one associates with ultra-Ortho-
dox sects.

The other researcher, Aahhotep Elouan, was a rangy, slender
astrophysicist, an Egyptian approximately twenty years older than
her Israeli counterpart.

At the center of the facility stood some sort of machine, not
much larger than a Volkswagen Beetle. The device rested on a
platform with built-in rotors, rollers, and wheels, clearly designed
to enable it to revolve, rotate, adjust, position, and reposition itself.

Notwithstanding the weight of distractions that had descended
upon him over a period lasting now nearly a day, Bridges recognized the apparatus as a replica of the gadget the Shah had revealed to him hours earlier in the basement of the Green Palace at
the Sa'dabad complex of royal residences outside Teheran.

"It's the positron-emission muon ionic holographic tele-trans-porter," Bridges said to the Shah.

"I'm not surprised that you recognize it," Pahlavi said, "but I'm impressed that you remember its name."

"Me too," Bridges said.

"Is this one working?" the Shah asked the scientists.

Before they could respond, the Shah turned to Bridges. "Chaim here and Aahhotep are the geniuses who created this gizmo. Chaim is Israeli; Aahhotep is Egyptian."

"An Arab and an Israeli?" Bridges said. "A Muslim and a Jew?"

"Notwithstanding millennia of strife," the Shah said, "Muslims and Jews are longtime partners in the region. Together, we share far more than whatever separates us."

"Both faiths stipulate in their orthodoxy, for example," Aahhotep said, "that women cover their hair."

"Observant members of both cultures," Chaim said, "do not eat pork."

"You can just about keep kosher," Aahhotep Elouan said, "by eating halal."

"And vice versa," Chaim said.

"At their cores," Aahhotep said, "both religions discriminate against women. Among fundamentalist Jews and Muslims alike, for example, women cannot serve as clergy."

"The two nations," the Shah said, "have collaborated quietly for years, working together to engage a plethora of territorial initiatives."

"There are parties in both communities," Chaim Yitzkowitz said, "who would not sanction such cooperation. That's why, at least for the present, both governments keep our joint projects under wraps. Iran has been an ardent proponent of conciliation, though the Shah can't exactly announce that in a news conference." Tilting his head toward the Persian monarch, he said, "Right, Rez?"

"Fucking A," the Shah said, nodding. He turned to Bridges. "Isn't that how they would put it in America?"

Bridges hesitated for a moment.

"Yes," he said.

He did not say that, in America, they pronounce it not "fucking" but "fuckin'."

Since partnering with General Motors a decade or so earlier, Bridges had banished profanity from his vocabulary. For car sales, foul language struck him as a losing strategy. Thanks to decades of conversations with hometown friends and neighbors—his earthy Dixieland bandmates for example —he knew his fair—or unfair—share of dirty words.

"Sooner than people expect," the Shah said, "the various cohorts will come to consider collaboration, comity, and cooperation to be preferable to controversy, conflict, and confrontation."

"And those are just the Cs," the Egyptian said.

"Aahhotep and I developed this project together," Chaim said, "starting a few years ago when we met as Fulbright Scholars in Philadelphia at Drexel University."

"Drexel?" the Shah said. "That's a university? It sounds like a laundry detergent."

Bridges laughed. "If this Shah thing doesn't work out for you," he said to Reza Pahlavi, "you can retreat to your fallback position: standup comedy."

The Shah smiled. "Everybody loves a compliment," he said, "but from a master so accomplished as yourself, it is especially meaningful."

"The device utilizes trion," Chaim Yitzkowitz explained, "a quantum-bound state combining three charged particles."

"I see," Bridges said, nodding, though he saw nothing.

"Controlled dark ions," Aahhotep Elouan said, picking up the narrative, "in a semiconductor—in this instance ultra-inductive single-layer tungsten diselenide—increase the capacity, and alter the forms, not only of digital data transmission but also material phenomena."

"Material phenomena," Bridges repeated, nodding slowly, as if he understood.

"For example, human bodies," Chaim Yitzkowitz said.

"A negative trion," Aahhotep Elouan said, "contains two anti-ions and one muon. Conversely, a positive trion contains two muons and one boson."

"One boson," Bridges said, as if it made sense to him. Isn't a boson, he wondered, a breed of buffalo? Hadn't he and his mother encountered an entire herd of them years back, while touring Yellowstone National Park?

"A boson," Chaim explained, "constitutes the vacancy of a muon in a semiconductor, which causes it to behave in the manner of a charged particle."

Bridges nodded yet again, narrowing his gaze as if engaging the heft of the explanation, when, for all he understood, they could have been speaking Erse.

"The bottom line," the Shah said, "is that this machine can transport bodies in the same way a telephone transports sounds."

"You can phone yourself somewhere?" Bridges asked. "You can travel from one place to another electronically, like in that old science fiction movie *The Fly*, which I saw some months ago, a late-night offering on Hoggzwallow Hollow's television station, Channel 34?"

"The original produced in 1958 with Vincent Price?" asked the Shah. "Or the 1986 remake starring Geena Davis and Jeff Goldblum?"

"I didn't know there was a remake," Bridges said.

"I have not seen *The Fly*," Aahhotep Elouan said.

"I've seen one or the other of them," said the Israeli. "The original or the remake. I'm not certain which. At a multiplex in Ashkelon. It was in English, with Hebrew subtitles."

"This is much bigger than phoning yourself somewhere," Aahhotep said. "This is no mere tele-transporter, not that there is anything 'mere' about tele-transportation."

She turned to the Israeli. "Chaim?"

"It's also a time machine," he said. "It can ferry you backward and forward in hours, years, even eons."

"And it can position you in two, or three, or any number of locations in this universe," Aahhotep said.

"Or any number of multiverses," Chaim said.

"All at the same time," the Shah said.

Bridges thought about that for a moment. "Wouldn't that make it possible to rearrange history?"

"Rearranging history," Shah Reza Pahlavi said, "is what historians have been doing since the beginning of history."

For a moment, nobody said anything.

"You must be anxious to get home," the Shah said at last to Bridges. He turned to the scientists. "Can you reconfigure the tele-transporter's settings for Mr. Ritchie's residence?"

"Piece of pie," Aahhotep Elouan said.

"Cake," Bridges said.

"Sorry?" the Egyptian said.

"Piece of cake," Bridges said.

"You desire a sweet?" the Shah asked Bridges.

"No thanks," Bridges said. "It's just an expression. Not pie. Cake. Piece of cake. Get it?"

"Fucking A, " the Shah said, nodding as if he understood, though Bridges had his doubts.

Aahhotep Elouan stepped up to a control panel. She fiddled with a multitude of potentiometers. Now she grasped a blood-red knob approximately the size of a clenched fist.

"Don't I need to prepare?" Bridges asked.

"For tele-transportation," the Shah said, "there's no way to prepare."

The Egyptian scientist twirled the knob.

The apparatus lurched in place.

Now it bucked like a bronco at the Doddridge County fair.

Next, it stirred and vibrated, as had its clone hours earlier at the royal Green Palace outside Teheran.

A shadow of dismay crept across the Shah's face. He turned to the scientists.

"You're sure this thing is working?"

"You needn't worry, Rez," Chaim said. He turned to Bridges. "We'll have you 'home' in a moment, Mr. Ritchie." He wiggled two fingers of each hand, indicating air quotes.

"Home, yes," Aahhotep Elouan said. "Home to—where else?"

She and Chaim and the Shah of Iran announced in unison, "Hoggzswallow Hollow, West Virginia!"

The three burst into peals of laughter. Their shoulders shook. Tears ran down their cheeks. Ribbons of phlegm flowed from their nostrils.

Regaining his composure, the Shah said, "Mr. Ritchie is waiting."

The Egyptian stepped forward and attenuated some dials on the contraption's control panel.

The machine's pulsation intensified, evolving now into something of a rattle. There was the sound of gears striving and failing to mesh, somewhat like a car—for example a new or used Buick— that had thrown a connecting rod linking the piston to the reciprocating rotation of the crankshaft and its interlocking cams.

The Shah grew apprehensive, as if expecting the device to erupt in a hurricane of shrapnel.

Bridges shared his concern.

The laboratory filled with smoke, which grew denser by the second.

Soon it was impossible to see anything at all.

Lost in the murk, Aahhotep Elouan flailed blindly at a bank of switches.

At last, the device settled down, and the haze lifted.

The machine's door slid open.

Inside the chamber, leaning against the wall, was a Remington Model 870 Express Super Magnum hardwood pump-action shotgun.

Beside it, coughing and wiping her eyes, stood Mother Bridges.

CHAPTER
16

U pon being booked into the Braxton County jail in nearby Chapmanville, the boys were promptly released on their
own recognizance.

Alvin Henderson drove the police cruiser back to Congregation
B'nai Ohev Shalom. On the front seat beside him, enclosed in
a clear plastic envelope from the evidence locker, lay Dwight
Bridges's paint-splotched ratty lambswool sweater.

As he pulled up to the temple, he could see Rabbi Sol Geffner
kneeling beside janitor Patterson, the two of them scrubbing away
at the last of the crudely painted epithets.

"Wait!" Henderson called, leaping from the car and racing toward the pair, who looked up at him in confusion. "Don't!"

Slowly, painfully, the rabbi unfolded his frame and rose to his
feet. "You don't think we should eradicate these slurs with all de-
liberate speed?" he said in a singsong, rising and falling inflection.

"We should let our sanctuary stand sullied, a monument to ethnic and religious enmity?"

He heaved a Jewish sigh.

"Go figure," janitor Patterson said.

"The paint—it's gone? All of it?" Henderson asked. "You got all of it?"

The police officer bit his lip.

"If it makes you happy," the rabbi said, "or even if it makes you unhappy, there is still a remnant left, which we haven't yet erased."

Clearly relieved, peace officer Henderson removed a second evidence envelope from the car. The rabbi led him around the temple's corner to a wall stained with the partially expunged tag: *Dump Kiss* …

Should have done this earlier, Henderson told himself.

From his pocket, he withdrew a jackknife.

I'm a jerk not to have done this sooner, he thought. Should have done it first thing.

Damned shoddy police work, he reprimanded himself in silence.

Deploying the blade, he scraped away carefully at the *D* in *Dump* …

"Scraping with a knife mars the surface, Al," the rabbi said. "We find benzene and a soft-wire steel brush does the trick."

"I'd like to help you clean it up, Sol," Henderson said, brushing flecks of paint into the evidence bag. "Truly I would. Unfortunately, I've got police business to attend to."

"Of course," the rabbi said. "I only hope it's something more important than a harmless prank, overaged adolescent good ol' boys, way out in the boonies, getting into mischief, scrawling slogans on an anonymous structure."

Henderson held the bag aloft and peered at it closely, making sure that he had a sufficient sample.

He retreated to the car.

"This structure is hardly anonymous, Rabbi," Henderson said through the driver's window after settling in behind the wheel. "It has a name. 'Congregation B'nai Ohev Shalom.' It is a shrine, a holy sanctuary designed for celebration, worship, and spiritual devotion. If folks want other folks to respect their faith, folks have to respect other folks' faith."

The police officer turned the ignition key, dropped the car into gear, and drove off. As it sped away, the Crown Vic's tires produced a high-pitched yip, which was uncharacteristic for a vehicle driven by Officer Alvin Henderson.

Rabbi Solomon Geffner and janitor Melville Patterson watched the car grow smaller in the distance.

They turned to look at each other.

The janitor shrugged.

He said, "Go figure."

CHAPTER
17

The Schlomowitcz Center rose like a tiered fortress of annealed, case-hardened stucco undergirded by a latticework of rebar braced by tensile-strength steel. If a nuclear bomb went off in its face, all of Pasadena, all of Southern California, would be obliterated, but the Schlomowitcz Center would stand there unscathed.

Ferns, ivy, succulents, and potted palms sprouted from multilevel recessed walkways, girdling the otherwise brutalist edifice with a lush necklace of life. With its upscale landscaping and pedestrian pathways, the complex could have passed for a shopping mall designed by Albert Speer, except for the poured-concrete menorah with its eternal blowtorch flames scorching an Old Testament motto carved in Hebrew.

In keeping with the lavish attention visited upon him to this moment, there was nothing modest about the reception awaiting Bridges: bands, bleachers, barricades, balloons. The motorcade, mowing a swath across all four lanes of Colorado Boulevard, finally pulled up to the entrance. There, handlers extricated Bridges from the lead limo, steering him past crowds of pols and dignitaries eagerly awaiting their glimpse of the celebrated American humorist.

His escorts ushered Bridges through a side entrance, then down a spiral staircase, and finally up again into the building's somber interior. At this point, the chaperones departed.

Bridges stood alone in an eerily silent chamber.

After some time—seconds? A month?—a door slid open and then closed. Though Bridges saw no one enter, a veiled figure seemed to materialize before him from out of the ozone.

The individual swayed from side to side, then rocked up and back in place.

Bridges looked on in bewilderment.

"Will you join me in reciting the kaddish?" Rabbi Shirley Shapiro, thirty, asked Bridges.

Her brow was appropriately furrowed in the manner not only of rabbis but generic clergy in full-tilt contemplative mode. Hairpins secured a skullcap atop her head. A blue-and-white striped tallit, the traditional Jewish prayer shawl, lay draped across her shoulders.

"Kaddish?" Bridges asked.

The only association he could muster was kaddish cheese.

"A mourner's prayer," the rabbi said. "You've never heard of it? A hymn in praise of God."

"I'm not Jewish," Dwight Bridges told her.

"Neither am I," the rabbi said.

"You're not?" Bridges had assumed that all rabbis were Jewish.

"The suffix *ish* suggests *sort of*," Rabbi Shirley Shapiro said. "If you make a date to get together with someone at, say, sixish, it means approximately six o'clock. Maybe a little earlier. Maybe a little later."

The rabbi paused to let it all sink in.

"I am not approximately a Jew," she said. "I'm not sort of a Jew. I am wholly and completely a Jew. Every hair on my head, every cell of my body, every aspect of my essence is shaped by my identity as a Jew."

"But isn't 'Jew,'" Bridges said in a reluctant whisper, slightly choking on the word, "a slur?"

"Only when used as a modifier."

"A modifier? You mean like an adjective?" Bridges recalled Miss Cooper's fifth grade class at Stonewall Jackson Elementary on West Kittredge Road, thirty-something years earlier.

"Exactly," the rabbi said.

"So it's no insult to call someone a Jew?"

"Depends who's talking. If it's a Jew hater, yes. If not, not."

Bridges mulled that over.

"Understand?" the rabbi asked.

Bridges nodded and said, "I understand-ish."

"Understand-ish!" Rabbi Shapiro burst into laughter. "That is pure Richie Ritchie!"

With the corner of her shawl, she dabbed at her eyes.

How had Bridges come to find himself underground in Pasadena, California, with a rabbi—a woman, no less—exploring Talmudic issues? Adjusting to the light, or to the lack of light, Bridges studied his companion closely. Oddly enough, he recalled the musicians Arlene, Marlene, Charlene, and Darlene. Though swathed in an abundance of fabric, the rabbi cut a figure somehow as voluptuous as that of the Vegas virtuosi.

"We Jews are an opinionated people," Rabbi Shapiro said, "which is very much to our credit." She paused for a moment, partly to let Bridges consider what she had said, and partly to catch her breath. "There is a saying: 'Two Jews, three opinions.'"

"I've heard that," Bridges said.

"It isn't true."

"No?"

"It's two Jews, three hundred opinions."

She allowed Bridges a moment to consider what she had said.

"We love to argue," the rabbi continued. "All the same, there is one tenet upon which all agree."

She peered into Bridges's eyes, clear through to the back of his skull, as if to determine whether or not he was properly braced for insight so colossal, so freighted with impact, as to augur whiplash or a stroke.

At last she said, "If your mother's a Jew, you're a Jew."

She allowed Bridges time to consider the proposition.

The erstwhile West Virginia auto dealer was certainly perplexed by many of life's riddles, but one thing he knew for certain was that his mother was no Jew. Mother Bridges was a faithful member of Pastor Pete's congregation at Mt. Zion Baptist Assembly of God in Hoggzswallow Hollow, West Virginia.

Bridges now found himself wondering, however, about the *Zion* part.

"Do wretched, petty sinners choose an all-knowing, all-powerful ruler of the universe," the rabbi asked, "or is it the other way around?"

She let Bridges think about that for a moment.

"You don't choose your god," the rabbi continued, "as you might, say, a plumber, or brand of toothpaste."

She nodded to herself as if satisfied the matter was settled. From the expression on her face, however, Bridges could see that it was an issue she would ponder unto eternity.

"As Jews do not decide to be Jews," the rabbi continued, "neither do women nor men determine their route along God's highway. I had no more say in becoming a rabbi, for example, than you had in becoming the world's most popular comedian."

"But that's just it, Rabbi, don't you see?" Bridges explained. "I'm not a comedian."

"Oh my," she said, clinging to her composure with both hands and feet.

"The plain and simple truth, Rabbi, is that I'm a ..."

"I know," Shirley Shapiro said, no longer able to suppress her laughter. "A Buick dealer, am I right?" Before Bridges could confirm that she was right, she said, "Buicks. New and used. From— how does it go?—Hoggzswallow Hollow, West Virginia. Did I get it right? Did I?"

The rabbi rocked back and forth, not davening but laughing. The greater her effort to maintain control, the more copious the tears streaming down her cheeks. She wobbled and trembled where she stood. Fearing that she might fall dead away to the floor, Bridges reached out and clutched her elbow in support.

Now laughter poured out of her without restraint.

Soon enough she was dabbing again at her eyes with the corner of the tallit.

CHAPTER
18

O fficer Alvin Henderson avoided the McDonald's directly across the courtyard from the FBI Regional Forensic Medicine and Legal Toxicology Center in Richmond and sat alone instead at the counter of a greasy spoon down the street. The place was called Lil's, even though the proprietress—fifty, narrow atop and broad in the beam—was named Beverly.

Henderson watched Beverly deep-fat-fry the burger patty. Now she stuffed it into a bun and slathered it generously with a rust-colored sauce of indeterminate origin.

The lawman acknowledged his anti-franchise bias. He felt duty bound, not only as a citizen but as a peace officer, to support independent entrepreneurs wherever and whenever he could, even if he regarded the Big Mac as one of the greatest achievements in the history of Western Civilization.

He bit down on the coal-black outside, frozen-raw inside, rancid-with-grease-everywhere burger.

He put it back on his plate.

"Everything okay, hon?" Beverly chirped, prissy and perky like an early teen.

"Absolutely," Henderson said. As a courtesy, he took another bite of the sandwich, struggling to mask his revulsion.

At the same moment, in Hoggzswallow Hollow, the Channel Six newsmobile sat parked outside the annex to the county courthouse. The annex was several times larger than the courthouse itself.

Inside, for lack of anything better to do, a dejected Wilbur Morton monitored the proceedings and nonproceedings, wondering what he was doing in a jerkwater place like Hoggzswallow Hollow. He longed for reassignment to some respectable cosmopolitan center, a metropolis with maybe even just a touch of hustle-bustle, a place where a television journalist could garner a modicum of attention and build a career.

With luck, maybe even Wheeling.

Just now, as usual, nothing newsworthy was underway before the bar. Couple of vagrancies, couple of outstanding traffic warrants, a disorderly conduct, a disturbing the peace.

These were not crimes.

They were not even misdemeanors.

They were mere infractions.

Wilbur leaned back and dreamed of murder and mayhem, riots, looting, arson, chaos, scandal.

His ears perked up when Ezra Convy and the two Baker brothers entered the courtroom, accompanied by Ez's lawyer, a shiny-suited youngster from the neighboring township of Buckhannon. Alas, however, considering the details presented during the arraignment, the Convy-Baker matter struck Morton as trivial. Appeared to be a mix-up, he surmised, pretty much as the lawyer claimed. Had the boys gotten into some sort of benign mischief? Committed a lame prank?

Wilbur knew that, in any event, he couldn't criticize Convy. He bought gas from the fellow at his Mobil station out on Old Deerfield. What would happen if he featured the story, and Ez got pissed?

These days, the last thing you wanted to do was piss off anybody who sold gasoline.

The county attorney was having a devil of a time framing his own arguments. Why, the magistrate asked him, should these men be charged with an unlawful act if the prosecution couldn't produce an aggrieved party, either at that Hebrew church, whatever they call it, or at Dwight Bridges's residence? Notwithstanding allegations that they had desecrated one property and broken and entered another, there was no evidence of any intent to wreck or raze either. The defendants had impeccable records, no records at all, really, except for the younger Baker, who'd once caught a firearms violation, plus a couple or three DUIs.

And where, the judge demanded to know, was Alvin Henderson, not only the arresting officer but also the complaining witness, the only party who could shed any light on the circumstances?

Wilbur Morton's attention drifted away from the proceedings.

He dreamed of assassination.

If Hoggzswallow Hollow could only come up with a decent assassination, Morton reckoned, even just one, that would be the kind of story a reporter could sink his teeth into. That was the kind of story the networks relished. It was a narrative that would enable a video newsman to forge a reputation. Where would that guy—what's his name?—Dan Rather be if Kennedy, the first Kennedy, hadn't been zapped at the time Rather just happened to be covering Dallas? If the Cubans, or whoever it was, hadn't shot JFK, who would ever have heard of Dan Rather?

Wilbur had tried to interest the networks in the caper at B'nai Ohev Whatever, hawking it as an angle that would link the national mood with the energy crisis.

No bites.

Strictly local stuff, the upper-ups told him. At best, regional. A wire service had gotten hold of the story, provoking a glimmer of attention in print, but the TV networks? They were too busy trolling mega celebrities like Telly Savalas, Jimmy Walker, Robby Benson, Sonny Bono, Charlene Tilton, and Jacklyn Smith.

Before the bench, the magistrate was doing all the work for the defense, so much so that Convy wondered why he was retaining this backwoods whippersnapper barrister in the first place.

If the county couldn't come up with a complainant, someone with standing, for example the Jewish preacher at the Hebrew church, or the residents of the violated premises, victims like Dwight Bridges or Mother Bridges, parties willing to press some sort of statutory grievance, he couldn't see charging the alleged perpetrators, let alone detaining them and setting bail. Granted, the circumstances were weird, but weirdness all by itself was no crime. Wasn't it the prosecutor's burden, after all, to show cause why the whole dang thing oughtn't be dropped?

"Dismissed," the justice announced.

Convy's attorney smiled broadly, winking at his clients.

Convy rolled his eyes. He thought, This fool thinks he's Clarence Fucking Darrow.

Surprisingly, Convy experienced a frisson of sympathy for poor old Alvin Henderson, who, after all, was only doing his job. To tell the sorry truth about it, Convy knew he had them nailed dead to rights. Plus, Henderson had squandered the chance to collect the easiest five hundred bucks any man in the Monongahela Valley had ever known.

I forgive him, Ezra Convy said to himself.

At that moment, Officer Alvin Henderson was driving far faster than any fifty-five. Lil's or Bev's or whoever's rancid burger still churning in the pit of his belly, he sped back from Richmond, where the FBI's regional forensics facility had performed some hurry-up lab work on his behalf.

Beside him on the passenger's seat lay two large envelopes. One contained Dwight Bridges's paint-stained ratty lambswool sweater. Alongside the garment was a folder with affidavits as to evidence, laboratory reports, and several microscopic glass slides.

Henderson drove up to the courthouse annex and tried to pull into one of the several spaces reserved for county vehicles, but all were occupied. He left the car, blocking the Channel Six newsmobile, and started for the steps when both Bakers, Convy, and their lawyer emerged through the door.

They were all smiles.

Close behind them marched Wilbur Morton.

"No hard feelings, Al," Convy said, encountering Henderson.

"None at all," the officer said.

"Don't say I didn't warn you come outta this looking a tad silly," Convy said.

"Wouldn't say nothing like that," Henderson said.

"What would you say," Convy said, "to a frosty, foamy *Rolling Rock* on me?"

Even in the crisp autumn air, a brew tempted Henderson. "Thanks, Ez, sounds good, but I can't take you up on that just now. I'm on duty. Can I have a rain check? Got some business needs tending."

"Nothing that can't wait?"

"Not likely. Got to make an arrest."

"That right?"

"Couple arrests. Three, in fact."

"Anybody I know?"

"You could say so," Henderson said. "Ez, it's yourself. Yourself, and those two Bakers, yonder."

The five of them—two Bakers, Convy, their lawyer, and Wilbur Morton—regarded Henderson with confusion.

"And that ain't all," Henderson said almost apologetically. "In absentia, I'm also swearing out a warrant against Dwight Bridges. I'm sorry to say I suspect Dwight was involved along with you other fellows."

"Not just Dwight," the younger Baker blurted.

"Shut up," Convy snapped.

"Well, it wasn't just Dwight and us, Ez," young Baker defended himself.

"Just shut up your mouth," Convy commanded.

"Well, how come Warren gets off scot-free?"

"Jam it. Slam it."

"Officer," the lawyer said to Henderson, "can you specify the nature of the charges?"

"Of course," Henderson said, nodding. "Illegal trespass, vandalism, defacement of a public facility, desecration of a religious shrine, also breaking and entering the Bridges residence, as well as conspiracy to commit all the aforementioned."

Wilbur Morton drank it all in.

He darted down the steps to the Channel Six newsmobile.

"Boys," Officer Alvin Henderson said, "you are under arrest. You have the right to remain silent. If you choose to speak, anything you say can and will be used against you in a court of law."

The arrestees and their representative stood there, numb.

"You have the right to an attorney," Henderson continued. "In the event you cannot afford an attorney, the court will appoint—"

"Hang on now," the lawyer said. "These gentlemen have an attorney."

"Hell we do," Convy said.

"Just take it calm now, Ez," the lawyer said. "And don't say anything. Let me do the talking."

"Talk to your dick," Convy advised his former attorney. "You ain't no lawyer of mine."

CHAPTER
19

Except for the lone Secret Service agent, dozing fitfully in a Kennedy rocker, the room was deserted. Thanks to resourceful interior decorating, no one would have suspected the chamber was buried a hundred feet underground.

It was an ultra-plush '50s-era fallout shelter.

Notwithstanding its homey, upholstered, wood-paneled layout, the cell was a fortress. For all its ease and comfort, it was capable of withstanding a multi-megaton nuclear blast.

At center stood a mahogany conference table surrounded by captain's chairs. Further back, churchlike pews lined all four walls. Scattered here and there were plush ottomans and a pair of burgundy leather sofas.

There was also a fully stocked bar.

The only clue regarding the location was the carpet.

Embroidered into its fabric was the image of an eagle, one set of talons clasping an olive branch, the other a clutch of arrows. A pennant streaming from its beak bore the legend: *E Pluribus Unum*.

It was the seal of the President of the United States.

Within arm's length of the chair at the head of the table was a control panel hosting an array of switches, toggles, dials, levers, rheostats, attenuators, and knobs.

Against the far wall stood a contraption approximately the size of a Volkswagen Beetle. The device rested on a platform with built-in rotors, rollers, and wheels, clearly designed to enable it to revolve, rotate, adjust, position, and reposition itself.

Suddenly, the mechanism lurched in place.

It hummed, rattled, and shook.

The agent sat up abruptly.

In a seamless sweep, his arm withdrew the government-issued 9mm Glock, which the U.S. Secret Service had recently distributed to its deputies, replacing the Sig Sauer .357 duty firearm, a move in keeping with the bureau's shift toward lighter, more efficient weaponry.

The device settled down.

All was silent and still.

Reassured that the perimeter had not been breached, the officer returned the weapon to its holster.

Yawning and stretching, he rearranged his frame in the chair.

Shutting his eyes, he resumed his nap.

Once again, the apparatus stirred, thrummed, and bucked.

The agent's eyes popped open.

His right hand reached again inside his jacket to his shoulder holster, withdrawing the Glock.

The machine shivered.

Its pulsation intensified, morphing into something of a rattle. There was the sound of gears striving and failing to mesh, like that of a car—for example a new or used Buick—that had thrown a connecting rod, linking the piston to the reciprocating rotation of the crankshaft and its interlocking cams.

The device settled down.

Handgun at the ready, the guard scanned the chamber.

His gaze focused on the machine.

It stood quiet and still.

The security agent arose from the rocker. His weapon trained on the apparatus, he circumnavigated it clockwise, then counterclockwise.

At last, he laid the gun on the table and lowered his frame into one of the overstuffed easies.

He yawned, stretched and, once again, closed his eyes.

He was resuming his snooze, when the apparatus began once again to hum.

The officer's eyes opened.

He retrieved the gun from the table.

The apparatus continued to purr.

A panel slid away, exposing its interior, a chamber approximately the size of a West Virginia backcountry outhouse.

Glock in hand, the deputy drew a bead upon two men jammed together in the cramped space. Disentangling their limbs from one another, Dwight Bridges and the Shah of Iran stepped from the device into the room.

CHAPTER
20

Rabbi Shirley Shapiro, still dabbing at her eyes with the corner of her clerical shawl, led Bridges through dark, windowless corridors, up and down stairways. Every so often she threw back her shoulders, thrust out her chest, and held her head erect. A sober rabbinical bearing would briefly descend upon her.

Within moments, however, her body once again trembled with poorly suppressed laughter. "Hoggzswallow Hollow," she rasped under her breath, shaking her head up and back in Ashkenazi angst.

They arrived at a dim landing with two heavy steel doors.

They paused.

"It's not fair for me to keep you all to myself," the rabbi told Bridges.

She indicated the door to the left.

As if impersonating TV game-show host Monte Hall, whose *Let's Make a Deal* reruns were available in syndication midafternoons via Hoggzswallow Hollow's Channel 34, she said, "Through Door Number One await members of the press and officials representing the city, county, and state. Through Door Number Two, however, lies a more circuitous route. It's a slight detour, which gives me five more minutes to show you some of our facilities. It also gives me a chance, frankly, to get a grip on myself so as not to appear a giggling fool when we encounter members of the press, the public, and the congregation."

"Whatever's your pleasure," Bridges said.

He wondered for the first time if he wasn't becoming acclimated to the firestorm of attention accompanying his newfound celebrity.

Over the hours, his attitude had evolved.

Had he come willingly, even eagerly to embrace the public's approval? In anticipation of greeting his admirers, did he now experience a certain fervor?

Whatever the answer, he could surely tolerate another few minutes alone with the fetching young cleric.

Rabbi Shirley Shapiro opened the second door.

She and Bridges stepped into a sizable enclosure whose walls were lined with ceramic tile. On the floor was an arrangement of drains. Set here and there along the area's perimeter, were porcelain-lined recesses, resembling grottos at a health spa.

Mounted high on the walls along the area's perimeter were a number of shower heads.

As they walked, the pair's footsteps reverberated like artillery.

Surveying the premises, a look of pious righteousness settled over Bridges's face. "I'm deeply moved," he whispered.

"You are?" the rabbi asked.

"Absolutely," Bridges replied. "I mean, the showers and all."

Rabbi Shirley Shapiro appeared mystified.

"The showers," Bridges said again. "The camps."

The rabbi offered no indication that she understood.

"The Holocaust," Bridges said.

"What?" Rabbi Shirley said.

After a moment, enlightenment descended upon her.

"Dear God, no. You don't understand," she said.

"But I do," Bridges said, nodding slowly, wholly deadpan. "The gas chambers at the camps with their mock showerheads, intended to lull the victims into complacency."

"No, no," Shirley Shapiro insisted gently. "This is a reform mikvah."

"Mikvah?"

"Ceremonial baths for women," the rabbi explained, "an ancient Jewish tradition. Here we've updated it. Think of it as a green mikvah. Instead of ritual baths, liturgical showers."

Bridges knew what *green* meant, but not *mikvah*.

"It is the embodiment of our new-age climatological consciousness," the rabbi continued, "our acknowledgment of environmental principles and issues."

Bridges, like no small number of his Hoggzswallow Hollow neighbors, was skeptical of purported "ecological considerations," which he saw as camouflage designed to conceal authoritarian overreach.

"Those fixtures, for example," the rabbi said, indicating the mirror-bright nozzles, "are flow-restricting, water-conserving spigots utilizing air-induction technology."

She paused to let Bridges process the data.

"We've conducted a cost-effective analysis," the rabbi continued, "and prepared an environmental-impact report. Did you know that the typical mikvah utilizes on average seventy-two gallons of water per congregant?"

Bridges acknowledged that he had not known that.

"Here," the rabbi continued, "we require merely eight."

Bridges nodded, feigning appreciation for the institution's commitment to preserving the planet's resources.

"Furthermore," Rabbi Shapiro continued, "in support of gender-neutrality in Torah and Talmud, we have mikvahs not merely for women but also for men. It's central to embracing a Judaism that is connected to the complexities of our present-day world. Our faith need not be entombed in long-ago-outmoded precepts that may have been appropriate at a different time in another place."

"Ceremonial showers," Bridges said quietly.

After a moment, he added involuntarily, as if the words just slipped out, "All that's missing are sacramental hair dryers."

Rabbi Shirley Shapiro shrieked with laughter that resounded throughout the corridor. "Sacramental hair dryers!"

She slid aside a frosted-glass panel, revealing a chamber featuring twin rows of gleaming aluminum hair dryers.

CHAPTER
21

By the time Wilbur Morton extricated his bulky handheld movie equipment from the Channel Six newsmobile, there wasn't a lot of material to shoot. Residents of Hoggzswallow Hollow who owned television sets—both of them—would be treated to blurry footage of Convy and the Bakers making their way back up the courthouse steps, to the accompaniment of Officer Alvin Henderson's pro forma statement.

"Three suspects have been arrested," Henderson said. "We seek two more. That's all I can tell you."

"What led to the arrests, Officer?" Wilbur asked.

"The case is before the court. Any comment I make could prejudice the rights of the defendants." He pronounced it as two separate words, "defend-dance," in that manner exclusive to law-enforcement personnel, the way cops pronounce "vehicle," for example, as "vee-hickle."

"Who are the two suspects still at large?"

Henderson disappeared through the courthouse annex doors.

Morton, his feet entangled in his cables, was stopped cold.

He was still struggling to liberate himself from the Gordian knot of coaxial when Henderson reappeared only moments later, exiting the structure, hunching his shoulders against the chill.

"Just tell us one thing," Morton pleaded, huffing and puffing as he struggled to keep up with the police officer. Viewers would be treated to a jiggling shot of Henderson's back descending the steps. "Tell us the names of the suspects who are still at large."

The policeman continued to recede.

The camera continued to trail him.

Henderson maintained his silence.

"Would it be Warren Robertson?" Wilbur called after Henderson. "Would it be Dwight Bridges?"

Henderson got into the county car, started the engine, and backed away. Wilbur stumbled alongside the driver's window. "Didn't one of those already arrested, one of the Baker brothers, didn't he mention Warren Robertson?" The car continued to slip backward, and Wilbur slipped with it. "Didn't you mention the Buick dealer Dwight Bridges? Is Dwight Bridges involved?"

The car pulled away.

Wilbur watched it depart, then turned the camera on himself, lofting it at arm's length, the lens peering back at its operator. Here was the progenitor of video selfies before there were videos, and before there were selfies.

He tried to think of something to say but couldn't come up with a single word.

He killed the camera's motor.

He collected his equipment and piled it into the clunker that was the Channel Six newsmobile.

Upon returning to the studio, he struggled once again to thread the film/video link and connect it to the network feed. Maybe up there in New York, some fellow at the flagship station, someone as bored and desperate as he, might find an angle, a fragment of an excuse—a human-interest item, small-town Americana—to run fifteen or thirty seconds of the footage.

It didn't seem likely.

CHAPTER
22

The Secret Service agent stood erect, his left hand on his hip, his right hand training the Glock on Dwight Bridges and the Shah of Iran.

"Don't shoot!" Bridges said.

"How did you secure ingress to this sector?" the officer demanded.

"Sorry?" Bridges asked. "What did you say?"

"How did you get in here?"

"We traveled via a positron-emission muon ionic holographic tele-transporter," the Shah explained.

"Of course!" the agent said, slapping his forehead with his free hand. "Why didn't I think of that?"

Years would pass before *The Simpsons* would air. In a parallel multiverse, however, in an alternative time and place where that had already occurred, the guard might have exclaimed, "Doh!"

Scanning the premises, the Shah said, "Surely this site cannot be our intended destination."

"There must be a glitch in the algorithm," Bridges said. "Apparently the unit is still in beta."

Glitch? Algorithm? Beta?

Not only was the security guard confused by what Bridges had said, but so also was Bridges. English was, after all, his mother tongue. It was also his mother's mother tongue.

"We arrived here by accident," the Shah said. "The transporter is clearly a work in progress. It shuttles people around in time and place, but sometimes not the intended time or place. It's as if you hail a cab in Manhattan at, just as a hypothetical, Lexington Avenue and 92nd Street. You instruct the driver to take you to, say, Riverside and West End. He drops you instead at, for example, the northwest corner of Christopher Street and Maiden Lane in the Greenwich Village or, I don't know, maybe even Steinway Street and 34th Avenue in Astoria, the Queens."

"Not *the* Queens," the security agent said. "Just Queens. There's the Bronx, okay, but with Queens it's only 'Queens.' Also, not 'the Greenwich Village,' just 'the Village,' or simply 'Greenwich Village,' without the 'the.'"

"Our handlers must have misdialed," Bridges said.

The Secret Service agent peered long and hard at the intruders. Now his demeanor appeared to shift.

He returned the handgun to its holster inside his jacket.

"I am Reza Pahlavi," the Shah told the security agent. Indicating Bridges, he said, "And this is—"

"You don't have to tell me who this is," the agent said, smiling at Bridges as if they were long-lost friends. "Everybody knows Richie Ritchie, a Buick dealer, new and used, from Hoggzswallow Hollow, West Virginia. Did I get that right?" Through a phlegm-rattling snort rooted in his trachea below the pharynx, the officer gurgled, "I caught your act at the Kick-ass Komedy

Klub in Cucamonga last October during your All-Star National Standup Tour, when my wife and I were visiting her second cousins, once removed, in Azusa."

After a moment, he added, "You killed!"

The security guard slid open a drawer and withdrew a sheet of stationery, official White House letterhead, with the presidential seal embossed at the top alongside a stylized rendering of the White House.

He thrust it at Bridges, along with a pen.

"If you don't mind," the agent said. "Otherwise my kids won't believe me when I tell them I've met you."

Bridges took the pen and paper from the agent. He scrawled *Best wishes.*

Now, he hesitated.

As if he were some other person, as if he were watching himself from across the street, or the distant shore of a lake, or the far side of an ocean, he signed: *Richie Ritchie.*

"Thanks so much," the agent said, accepting the document, delicately folding it, and placing it inside his jacket pocket.

"Of course I don't need any proof of your identity, Mr. Ritchie," the agent told Bridges. "Regarding this other gentleman, however," he said, indicating the Shah, "I require a photo ID."

The Shah of Iran stood there in silence. Never before had anyone asked him to present any kind of ID, photo or otherwise.

"As he's already told you, Officer," Bridges said, "he is Reza Pahlavi."

The Secret Service agent shrugged.

"He's the Shah of Iran," Bridges said.

"Sha Na Na," the agent said, invoking the oldies-but-goldies '50s doo-wop novelty act, "is the only Shah I know. Anyone can claim their name is—how did you put it?—Ray Somebody?"

How bizarre can life be? How do I come to find myself under-ground, Bridges wondered, ten stories beneath the White House, in the president's emergency command center?

Still more mysterious was his encountering here yet another stranger who seemed to know precisely who he was. A renowned world leader, on the other hand, an authentic icon of international repute such as the Shah of Iran—legendary to some, notorious to others, but recognizable across the planet—was an intruder, an anonymous trespasser required to present a photo ID.

"Never before in my life," the Shah said, "have I been asked to establish my identity."

"A passport will suffice," the Secret Service agent said.

"I am the king of Persia," the Shah said. "Kings don't carry passports."

"Then maybe a driver's license?" the guard asked.

The Shah shook his head.

"You don't have a driver's license?" the Secret Service man asked.

Again, the Shah shook his head.

The officer stood there in silence for another moment.

Now he asked the Shah, "How do you cash a check?"

CHAPTER
23

Rabbi Shirley Shapiro, still quietly chuckling, led Dwight Bridges from the ceremonial showers into a carpeted ante-chamber lined with lockers. They made their way along a stunted hallway that led to yet another steel door. The corridor was flooded with the aroma of fresh baking pastry, braised and marinated lamb, fish, poultry, sauces, steaming vegetables.

Bridges sighed. "I feel like I haven't eaten now for a hundred years."

"You've come to the right place," the rabbi told him.

She opened the door.

They entered the world's most deluxe cafeteria.

Far more than any self-serve canteen, with its Carolingian tapestries, teak tables, and Windsor chairs, the place resembled a medieval banquet hall. "We've got absolutely the finest chef in the universe. You've never tasted anything like her knishes, kasha, kneidlach, kreplachs, and kugel," Rabbi Shapiro said, "and those are just the Ks. She also does blintzes, latkes, tsimmes. We're talking the most scrumptious nosherei this side of Hester Street."

"Hester Street?"

"On New York's Lower East Side."

"Kishka?" Bridges asked. "Tsimmes?"

"Jewish delicacies. Did I mention that she also bakes the world's sweetest challah?"

"Challah?"

"That one you should know," the rabbi said. "Aren't you a Buick dealer from Hoggzswallow Challah?"

She laughed so hard at her own joke that it appeared to Bridges her yarmulke would come loose. He worried the rabbi would lose not only her skullcap but consciousness.

Reclaiming her composure, Rabbi Shapiro led Bridges past rows of tiered steam tables rising on both sides, like stadium seating at a sports arena. The boards groaned under the weight of appetizers the likes of which were unknown to him. "I wish there were time for a formal sit-down," the rabbi told him, "but there's a limit as to how long we can keep the press and public at bay."

She picked here and there at the array of morsels, passing one or another to Bridges. Ravenous, he swallowed each item whole.

"I know what you're thinking," Rabbi Shirley told Bridges.

Even Bridges did not know what he was thinking.

"You're thinking how inappropriate it is for us to feature so vast an abundance of comestibles at a Holocaust center."

A polite little burp—or maybe it was an inadequately suppressed fart, like one of those feigned earlier by Jerry Lewis during the public television panel debate—escaped her.

"Oops!" she said. "Excuse me. The last thing we need at an institution like this is gas."

Bridges laughed uneasily.

Could the extermination of millions of innocents properly serve as a subject for humor?

On the other hand, was Charlie Chaplin morally bankrupt for having made *The Great Dictator*, a farce mocking Hitler? Was it unconscionable for Mel Brooks, in an era that had not yet arrived, to stage *The Producers*, with its mellifluous anthem "Springtime for Hitler," not to mention a dancing swastika? And how about the aforementioned Jerry Lewis, whose largely ignored WWII comedy *Which Way to the Front* featured legendary Jewish character actor Sidney Miller playing The Führer? Or Roberto Benigni's Oscar-winning *Life is Beautiful*, a comedy set in a concentration camp modeled after Auschwitz?

How better to denounce Nazism than through ridicule and scorn?

Bridges figured the gas gag was probably acceptable from the rabbi, but not from him.

He had seen *The Great Dictator* on Hoggzswallow Hollow's Channel 34, a tattered print of which, spliced and spliced again, had somehow found its way into the station's modest film library. And he and his mother had also viewed part of the Jerry Lewis film on 34's *Weekend Funny Film Fest*, before turning it off in the middle of a soliloquy delivered by Jan Murray.

He had not yet seen *The Producers*, however, since it had not yet been produced.

Bridges hefted from the buffet a dumpling stuffed with ground veal. He popped it in his mouth and was transported instantaneously to flavor's Promised Land.

"The purpose of the Center is, first of all, to convey to people who know nothing of the Holocaust, that it happened," the rabbi said. "This commissary attracts people from the entire Southwest. The grub brings them in. Then we shuttle them off to the exhibits, libraries, archives, lectures, workshops, and rides."

Feeding his face, Bridges followed the rabbi to a door opening onto another stunted corridor. "Through here," Rabbi Shapiro explained, "is a shortcut to the sanctuary where you'll preside over the ceremony."

"Ceremony?" Bridges mumbled, his jaw working a portion of creamed pickled herring draped across a shard of organic, hormone-free, non-GMO, canonically correct, organic whole-wheat matzo.

"Right this way," the rabbi said, holding open yet another door.

The two of them moved into the gift shop, which was no larger than Costco would have been if, in that universe, during that era, there had been a Costco. At the moment, it was merely as large as, say, Fedco, or Adray's, or White Front.

Rising to the ceiling were shelves bearing merchandise: tees, sweats, sneakers, jogging suits, sun shades, hats, banners, mugs, each and every item prominently featuring the Schlomowitcz Center logo.

There were also books and magazines, from pamphlets to coffee-table tomes. The current issue of *Holocaust Monthly* stood beside stacks of *Holocaust Weekly*. Copies of *Genocide Journal* were piled beside *Genocide Review*. There were oversized editions of Holocaust photo books, some so substantial as to require two people to turn a page. Among them was *Above Auschwitz*, which provided aerial views of the death camp. It retailed for some hundred and sixty dollars and, as the inside cover flap advised, would rise to two hundred and ten in the new year, though it failed to specify which new year: Roman, Gregorian, or Hebrew.

The excitement was palpable among the staff in anticipation of the arrival of *Crimes Against Humanity Volume IV*. There were also stereopticon viewers featuring three-dimensional panoramas of Mauthausen and Treblinka.

Rabbi Shirley Shapiro paused at the main entrance. She looked down at a new issue of ashtrays and souvenir gas masks imprinted, again, with the Schlomowitcz logo. The rabbi picked up an armband bearing a yellow Star of David, and contemplated it wistfully. Bridges waited, patiently and respectfully. Now he saw a tear emerge from her eye, and she began gently to shudder. He held his breath, silently praying for the young woman to regain her composure.

The rabbi continued to tremble.

Out of concern for her safety, Bridges gently plucked her elbow. He whispered, "Are you all right?"

Instead of bursting into tears, Rabbi Shirley Shapiro burst into laughter.

CHAPTER
24

Breathing on the right side, and then the left, the swimmer stroked a remarkably fluid crawl.

Within the resounding chamber, she swam alone.

She was just completing her last lap when the door swung open.

Gingerly making their way along the slippery deck, the Secret Service agent led Bridges and the Shah of Iran to the shallow end. The swimmer came to a halt at the wall. Standing waist-deep in the water, she removed her goggles. Next, she pulled off her Lycra cap and shook loose her lush, lustrous mane.

Leaning over the edge of the pool, in the sort of judicious whisper reserved for royalty, the agent said, "Please forgive the intrusion, Madam President."

The swimmer gestured with her head, tilting it sideways toward a stack of towels. Each one, the size of a bedsheet, had stitched into it the Seal of the President of the United States.

"Towel me," she said.

The Secret Service agent plucked a towel from the pile.

The swimmer ascended a ladder. Clad in a black Amalfi classic two-piece, she accepted the towel.

She patted her face, then draped the towel over her shoulders.

She regarded the trio.

"Reza!" she said. "Richie Ritchie!"

"Sarah!" the Shah greeted her.

"I shouldn't allow people to barge in on you during your swim," the Secret Service agent said.

"No, Horace," she said. "You did the right thing."

Facing Bridges and the Shah, she said, "I need downtime every day to decompress from the stress that accompanies this job. Left to my own devices, my handlers worry I'll drown. Or order the invasion of, say, Somalia. Or pardon Harvey Weinstein."

"Harvey Weinstein?" the Shah asked.

"A lowlife from an alternative era and parallel universe," she said.

She continued toweling off from the swim.

"God bless Franklin Delano Roosevelt," she said. "Didn't he get us through the Depression and World War II? As far as I'm concerned, though, his singular achievement was installing this pool in nineteen-thirty-whenever, to provide aqua-therapy to treat his paralysis."

She dropped the towel to the deck.

The security officer plucked a fresh number from the stack and handed it to her.

"I've issued standing orders to my security detail," she continued. "If a party shows up whose stature is as lofty as that of Richie Ritchie, he's to be spared the standard protocols and admitted forthwith. Like when Elvis showed up at the White House, unannounced, during Nixon's first term. They just ushered him in. You don't bother Elvis Presley or Richie Ritchie for a photo ID."

"Or the Shah of Iran," said the Shah of Iran.

"Or the Shah of Iran," she said.

President Palin turned again to face Bridges. "Thanks for your support at the inaugural ball back in January, Richie. You killed!"

"My pleasure entirely," Bridges said, as if he had the faintest idea what she was talking about. Hesitating, he asked, "But isn't Richard Nixon president today?"

"In your universe, perhaps," the president said. "I'm guessing you traveled here from an alternative world and a substitute future via the positron-emission muon ionic holographic tele-transporter."

The Secret Service agent nodded knowingly.

Bridges and the Shah nodded too.

"We've got one here in the White House," the president said.

"Downstairs," the Secret Service agent said. "Way, way downstairs."

"Right, Horace," the president said. "In the bunker."

"I've got one in Teheran," the Shah said.

"In the White Palace," Bridges said, recalling his adventures earlier this very same day, if not in this very same universe.

"Green," the Shah said. "The Green Palace."

"Green," Bridges nodded. "I remember it was a palace of color, one color or another, where I first encountered the transponder."

"Transporter," said the Shah.

"Right," Bridges nodded. "Transporter."

"The Israelis have one squirreled away somewhere," the president of the United States said. "Jerusalem? Tel Aviv?"

"It's underground at an installation in the Sinai Desert," Bridges heard himself say.

"Mossad briefed my military guys regarding issues with the device," the president said. "Occasionally it misdials. Also, goosing its power to the max apparently compromises its field. Travelers no longer have to enter the device. Sometimes it processes people who are merely standing nearby. Their destination is up for grabs. It might take them to Bulgaria, or Bahrain, or Bayonne, and those are just the Bs, or any other location in our current universe, or to a slew of parallel others. And not only that. It also delivers travelers to alternative time frames."

"I see," Bridges said, nodding as if he understood.

"Your preeminence is so monumental as to transcend even parallel universes," the president said to Bridges. "Given your origin, your locus in time and space on another astral plain, in this moment, in this universe, you have no idea who I am," she said. To you, Richie Ritchie, I must be a total stranger."

"I get that you're the president of the United States," Bridges said.

"For a month I was merely vice president. In the election, my running mate was a white guy from Arizona, a Vietnam war vet, a downed Navy Pilot, a national hero who had been captured by the enemy, tortured, and locked up for years in a prison camp. Even with a Catholic leading the ticket, and a woman running for vice president, defeating an Afro-American with an Arabic name was easier than tying your shoes. Apparently in this universe, at this moment, the American people are not ready to elect a leader who is multiracial."

The chief executive continued to towel off as she spoke.

"I was veep until the president, on a diplomatic mission, a state visit to Silesia—wherever that is—dropped dead of a heart attack or a stroke or something. Maybe it was diverticulitis. Had the election gone the other way, had there been an upset, an October surprise of historical proportions, we would have had the first president of color instead of me, the first president of female."

She reached out and clasped Bridges's hand.

Gesturing toward the Shah, she said, "Thanks to Reza's prom-
inence, given his stature in world history, seems like he and I
have known each other forever. Our paths have crossed now on a
number of political and diplomatic occasions, in a hodgepodge of
locales, scattered eras and multiverses. Am I right, Rez?"

"Right," said the Shah. "You are right."

She let the second towel fall to the deck, where it joined its
recently abandoned sibling.

"Horace?"

"Madam President?"

"Robe me."

The security guard lifted a bathrobe from where it lay draped
across a grab rail and handed it to the President

It, too, had embroidered into it the presidential seal.

Donning the garment, the president asked Bridges and the
Shah, "You guys up for a glass of wine or a beer or a sandwich or
something? The kitchen is open all night. Perhaps a little reefer?
Here and now it's contraband, but in parallel universes, in other
eras, it's legally sanctioned."

She cinched up the bathrobe's belt.

"We Muslims shun alcohol, thanks," the Shah said. "Regarding
reefer, earlier in the day I had a taste of hand-rolled copper
Nepalese temple hash, so in that regard, I'm good."

"Copper Nepalese?" the president said. "That one I never
heard of."

"It's made by gently sieving dried cannabis buds that are sifted
through fine-mesh screens."

"You don't say?" said the president.

"The gentle friction helps separate the trichomes into a fine
powder known as kief," the Shah continued. "This is then pressed
into blocks."

"Sounds nice," said the president.

"Righteous," the Shah said, nodding. After a moment he added, "Mellow."

"Without weed in my home state, we'd never survive winter's boredom. What kills you in Alaska is not the chill but the tedium. Even for the sled dogs running the Iditarod, the mushers lace into their kibble a few nuggets of indica."

"I did not know that," said the Shah.

"I didn't know that either," Bridges said.

"Is there any chance you could scare me up a cup of coffee?" the Shah said. "Decaf, if you have it?"

"It's a done deal," the president said. "Cream? Sugar?"

"No sweetener, thanks," the Shah said. "Cream is good, but do you have milk?"

"Of course we have milk," she said. "I'm the president of the United States. This is the freaking White House."

"Whole or skim?"

"Skim we got," the president said. "Whole? We got. Two percent milk fat? We got."

"Madam President," the Secret Service agent said, "I'm afraid the pantry is out of skim. I'll send someone to the 7-Eleven on Connecticut Avenue NW."

"Not to worry," said the Shah of Iran. "Two percent will do."

Compromise had been achieved, and the matter was settled.

"I've already told you how I love this pool," the president said. "But the rest of the White House? A dump. Talk about mildew! The upside is that the kitchen operates twenty-four/seven."

The surface of the pool, which had settled to a glassy mirror, now started to roil. Before everyone's eyes, the turbulence ratcheted up. In another moment, the water heaved with waves large enough to surf.

"What's going on?" the president asked the security guard.

"I don't know," Horace said, alarmed.

"Earthquake?" the president asked. "Invasion?"

"It's anybody's guess," the Secret Service agent said. "Respectfully, Madam President, regarding your safety, and for the security of the nation, we can't play guessing games."

The water was now sloshing over the deck.

He turned toward the two men. "Mr. Shah," he said, "Richie Ritchie." He turned back to the enrobed commander in chief. "Madam President. Please allow me to escort you to the bunker. Security protocols require us to proceed there with the utmost dispatch."

He was starting to corral the trio and lead them away, when the water grew suddenly tranquil.

Across the way, at the far end, blinking and sputtering, hair and apparel drenched, fluid draining from her body, climbing a ladder to the deck, there appeared the Egyptian astrophysicist Aahhotep Elouan.

She turned back to the pool.

Breaking the surface of the water, there emerged below her the butt end of a dripping-wet firearm. As it rose from the water, it could be seen for what it was, a Remington Model 870 Express Super Magnum hardwood pump-action shotgun.

Wielding it was a soaking-wet woman of late middle age.

She reached up and handed the sopping weapon to Secret Service Agent Horace, who set it down on the deck.

The Egyptian took hold of her companion's hand, supporting her as she climbed the ladder.

Bridges's eyes grew as wide as Frisbees.

"Mother!"

CHAPTER
25

In New York City, in television network offices perched nose-bleed-high in the stratosphere, it was not a slow-news but no-news day. In the central editorial suite, the staff monitored various regional feeds, combing through a potpourri of stories in search of something worthy for the nightly edition.

There was a pointless vignette regarding a family farm in one of the Dakotas that cultivated kiwi in a greenhouse; a listless account of salmon-fishing in the Pacific Northwest; the cobwebbed reminiscences of an obscure baseball old-timer who had donated his stamp collection to a junior high school in Cedar Rapids.

Even the gas-crisis stories were wearing thin.

There was a limit, after all, to how long viewers could tolerate footage of queued-up cars and screwed-up drivers. Lamentably, from the point of view of the newsmen, there hadn't been a decent gas-line shootout in several days, unless you counted a grandma in Lima, Ohio, who had threatened an attendant with a water pistol.

In that era, in that universe, service stations were still just that. They provided service. They pumped gas for you, cleaned your windshield, checked the oil and the tire pressure.

Happily, the crunch was beginning to abate, which fact caused Gerald Dorsett, a too-slick-for-his-own-good copy editor, to despair. Dizzy with boredom, his chin resting against his chest, he scanned the regional feeds across a multitude of monitors. In his late twenties, for a network comer, Dorsett was already over the hill. If he couldn't glom onto some scorching new story in a hurry, a fresh angle on something, anything, he knew he'd be hawking hot pretzels on the Avenue of the Americas.

At the moment, the only item of interest was the Pasadena feed, coverage of superstar standup comic Richie Ritchie, flogging his shy, self-effacing, what-me-worry shtick. Oddly enough, however, the comedian was about to deliver a speech commemorating the Holocaust. This new bit, a Holocaust number, might well provoke controversy. But wouldn't it have been designed for precisely that purpose? The performer's trademark naiveté would somehow render it tolerable, even respectable.

Newsroom phones buzzed and buzzed again, continuing to distract Dorsett. Caught up in the Pasadena feed, the rest of the staff stood by for Richie Ritchie's appearance, leaving it for somebody else to respond. Finally, a voice of superior rank called out, "Get that, will you, Dorsett?"

Gerald Dorsett grinned his freeze-dried grin. If he smiled broadly enough, he imagined, maybe they'd promote him to chief operating officer.

He seized the phone and said, "Newsroom."

Listening to the caller, the expression on his face grew skeptical.

"That for me?" the supervisor called out from the pack huddled around the Pasadena transmission.

"It's some dork," Dorsett said, not bothering to cover the mouthpiece, "some ninny hustling a feed from a UHF affiliate in Virginia, or West Virginia, or East Virginia, or North Virginia, one of them Virginias."

"What's the story?" the news director asked Dorsett.

"Another oil-crisis angle," Dorsett answered. "Apparently the sheriff arrested some good ol' boys who, blaming the Jews, painted some swastikas on a synagogue."

The news director thought about it. "The gas crisis is old news by now, but racism and religious bigotry always lead. Jewish issues in particular. Why, just look at Richie Ritchie and his whole new genocide number."

Gerald Dorsett held onto the phone, his prefab smile firmly in place. "Wouldn't running this footage just plant dumb ideas in the minds of additional morons?" he asked. "Do we want to promote religious vandalism?"

"Where'd you say the feed is from?" the executive inquired. "Virginia?"

"West Virginia," Dorsett answered. He looked down at some notes he had scribbled on his desk. "Hoggzswallow Hollow."

"Seriously? Did you say Hoggzswallow Hollow, West Virginia?"

CHAPTER
26

Amidst flashing strobes and cranking cameras, side by side with Dwight Bridges, Rabbi Shirley Shapiro strode the red carpet up to the foot-thick East Indian rosewood doors.

They paused briefly.

The rabbi placed her hand in the crook of Bridges's arm.

In the distance, just beyond the grand portal, was the buzz of several thousand devotees.

The doors swung open.

Stepping forward, the couple was greeted by a collective intake of breath.

This was followed by a silence so profound as to drown out the hum of traffic on Colorado Boulevard.

As the pair advanced into the high-ceilinged sanctuary with its ranked mahogany pews, somebody plopped a silk skullcap onto Bridges's head. An ovation arose. Like a storm tide surging toward shore, people rose to their feet as the procession passed. The reception morphed into a frenzied roar, a virtual riot that threatened to rend the chamber's walls.

The rabbi guided Bridges to a spiral staircase leading to the pulpit. By the time they arrived at the platform overlooking the congregation, he was short of breath.

Rabbi Shapiro stepped back a respectful distance.

Bridges stood alone at the forefront of the thunderous tribute. For a period as long as the Pleistocene Epoch, all he could do was nod, smile, and wave in acknowledgment of the adoration raining down upon him.

It seemed the ovation would never cease.

Eventually, Rabbi Shapiro stepped forward and stood again at Bridges's side. With a raised hand, she signaled the audience for silence.

The clamor gradually subsided.

The rabbi incanted a few Hebrew words of prayer and then turned to an elderly man standing among a cluster of dignitaries at the rear of the cramped platform. He handed her a tightly wound papyrus cylinder. She broke the seal and unfurled the document.

She held aloft before the crowd the elegantly hand-lettered scroll.

All regarded the parchment with awe, as if it were God's original draft of the Torah.

Clearing her throat, the rabbi read aloud.

"In recognition of his deep-rooted devotion to the human comedy and its life-affirming spirit," she intoned reverentially, "on recommendation of the Trustees, Elders, and Stakeholders of the Schlomo and Schanndah Schlomowitcz Holocaust Center, I confer upon Richie Ritchie the degree of Doctor of Holocaust Letters, with all rights, privileges, honors, and marks of distinction which pertain everywhere thereto."

She handed Bridges the diploma.

Lordy, Bridges thought, regarding the richly illuminated certificate with its gold-embossed calligraphy, this item cost a couple of bucks, let me tell you that. His attention was taken now by resurging applause from the audience in the pews and the dignitaries on the platform. Looking up from the diploma, he offered the crowd a modest half smile, nodding tentatively in one direction and now in another.

He offered a what-the-hey shrug.

The audience rushed the stage.

Lights flashed. Horns blared. Firecrackers crackled. There was a blizzard of confetti. People cheered and howled and hollered, declaring their devotion, professing their allegiance, their veneration, their faith.

Bridges stood there, waiting for the storm to subside. He recognized that he was obligated to offer some remarks. He scratched around inside his jacket for the pages manager Buddy Scheib had handed him on the plane, but came up blank. A quiet panic settled over him like the mist of a West Virginia morning. He was scheduled to speak, and hadn't a clue as to what he might say.

Eventually, the crowd shouted itself hoarse, and the tumult ebbed.

"So what can I tell you?" Bridges asked.

The humble query spawned a renewed flurry of approbation.

Bridges waited until the uproar dwindled to a subtle thrum.

"Naturally, I'm honored," Bridges said. "I don't have to tell you that I am flattered. And pleased. And happy, and delighted, and all those things. I don't have to tell you. What seems wonderful to me," he continued after a moment's quiet reflection, "what seems particularly wonderful, is that you honor today not some fancy philosopher or intellectual, or rocket scientist or brain surgeon or whatever, one of these mathematics guys or a famous historian or athlete or vegetarian—not that those fellows aren't deserving of your praise, I'm not putting them down—but what strikes me as significant today is you honor not one of those normally honored and honorable characters, one of these run-of-the-mill-type honorees, but a simple fellow like myself, a normal, regular, garden-variety American."

The audience ate it up.

"See," Bridges continued, "our nation's populated by all sorts of people, and among them are these guys I talked about, art painters, sculpture sculptors, literature writers. Outstanding folks, every one of them. But America's not mainly made up of those people. No. She's made up of steelworkers and truck drivers and janitors and plain human beings with no prospect of getting rich or famous or whatever, window washers, gas-station attendants, women and men working at dry-cleaning establishments, hamburger stands, what have you."

The hall settled down.

"Take me, for instance," Bridges said.

Nobody cried out, "Take him, please! Somebody! Anybody!"

"What do I know from any Holocaust?"

He peered long and hard at the congregation.

After pausing to gather his thoughts, Bridges continued. "Hebraic people, that is to say your Jews, have reason to rejoice. What reason? This reason, that reason. Mainly, perhaps, that they survive. I get it that, from time to time, throughout history, strategies are launched to annihilate them. Still, they endure. This building in which we gather reminds us of monstrous monstrosities perpetuated and perpetrated against them by hate-mongering monsters. Their ultimate strength, though, is their strength. Even as they must never forget their lost brothers and sisters, parents and grandparents, cousins, aunts and uncles, it's also a mistake to assign rage, horror, and grief the central role in life. Folks shouldn't allow their tormentors to split them into factions, blocs, sects, cults, whatever. Oppression ought not divide families but unite them.

We must reject the calculus of competitive suffering. Human be-ings are not contestants in some sort of affliction sweepstakes."

A pin-drop silence filled the hall.

"Anger," Bridges continued, "is often an appropriate emotion. There's plenty to be angry about. Unlike gasoline at a service station, you'll never have to wait in line for your ration of rage. Anybody not angry about one thing or another in this universe, or in any parallel universe or multiverse, whatever that may mean, is blind, brain-dead, or both."

Bridges paused for a ponderous moment.

"Outrage is a natural aspect of the human condition, he con-tinued at last. "Under the right circumstances it can even be empowering. It can fuel movements for social justice. But anger must not be the center, the organizing principle of a movement, or a personality, or a cause, or a campaign. Anyone who's seen Star Wars knows that love is stronger than hate," Bridges said, citing a movie that would not be produced for another three or four years. "Why, look at all you people cheering your love for me right now."

Bridges took a sip of water from a glass stationed on the podium.

"So what do I know from any Holocaust? Better you should ask me about the Hoggzswallow Hollow-cost," he said.

A swell of tittering roiled the room.

"After all, who am I?" Bridges continued. "I'm one single fellow, name of Dwight Bridges ..."

"Richie! Richie! Richie! Richie!" the crowd chanted.

"... a Buick dealer, new and used, from ..."

"... from Hoggzswallow Hollow ...," the audience shouted in approximate unison.

"... wallow Hollow," Bridges struggled to continue.

"... zswallow, low, low," the audience echoed.

"... low, West Virginia," Bridges concluded.

"... zswallow, low, low, West Virginia, gin ya, gin ya ya ya ..."

The hall went crazy.

Euphoria took hold of everyone within a fifty-mile radius of Pasadena.

Pressed by the hordes behind them, people at the front of the sanctuary swarmed the security personnel stationed at the foot of the staircase leading to the pulpit. Propelled by the force of the mob, a dozen frenzied souls scrambled up the steps.

"… Gin! Ya! Gin! Ya!" all shrieked.

They seized Bridges and plunked him upon a chair, which four brawny men then lofted high in the air. As at a Jewish wedding, in wanton exultation they paraded Bridges about the territory, transporting him down the steps, up the aisle, into the corridors, and out into the glorious Southern California sunshine.

Bridges bounced and bobbed atop the chair, holding on for dear life.

"… Gin! Ya! Gin! Ya! Gin! Ya!" the crowd chanted like Haredi rapturously exalting the Lubavitcher redeemer Rebbe Menachem Mendel Schneerson of righteous memory.

CHAPTER
27

The Kings Cross pieces, carved from camel bone, stood at attention on the Mark of Winchester board, perched precariously on the nightstand at the head of the bed. The black squares were authentic ebony, the reds rare Brazilian cherry wood.

Through the floor-to-ceiling one-way window, the action out on the field was clearly visible. Wielding his thirty-three-inch Rawlings custom club, Dodger third baseman Billy Cox stepped into the batter's box. He tapped first one shoe with the barrel of the bat, and then the other, dislodging clods of turf from among the cleats.

He settled into his stance.

Yankee reliever Allie Reynolds shook off catcher Yogi Berra's first two signs, then nodded at the third.

He commenced his windup.

In the stadium's Delta SKY 360 Luxury Suite, however, the lovers paid scant attention to what was happening on the field.

Three black pawns plus a bishop lay in repose on the table beside the board at one end. A captured white pawn rested at the opposite edge, alongside a defeated knight. One look would tell aficionado and novice alike that it was early in the match.

Mother Bridges surveyed the board.

Her flowered peasant's blouse lay draped across the back of a chair. North of her waist, she wore only a Pandora necklace, sterling hoop earrings, and a Maidenform lace longline bra.

Now she made her move.

Delivering her surviving knight to king's bishop six, she captured a second pawn. She removed it from the battlefield and set it on the table alongside its fallen comrades.

The Shah looked up at his adversary.

An Oxford slip-on dangled from the toes of one foot. Its partner lay upside down on the floor beside the bed. "Do you think it's wise to wage so aggressive a strategy," he said, "when we've not yet entered the midgame?"

"What I think, Your Excellency," Mother Bridges said, "is that you owe me another garment."

"Your horseman is now exposed on three fronts," the Shah said, shaking his head in disapproval. He reached down and peeled a Mack Weldon sock from his foot, letting it drop to the floor.

"A sock is a garment?" Mother Bridges asked him.

"What is it, if not that?" he said.

"When you took my knight," she said, "I removed not only a shoe but also the stocking."

"That was your choice," the Shah said.

He studied the board as a plastic surgeon might examine a burn victim, seeking a few good cells to start a graft.

At last, he pushed his king's rook's pawn two spaces forward, where it threatened an opposing pawn.

"The Caro-Kann Defense?" Mother Bridges said, nodding. "How can you imagine I'd fall for so obvious a trap?" Instead of snatching the pawn with her own, Mother Bridges moved her queen's rook one step forward.

The Shah advanced the pawn, seizing his opponent's counterpart. He set the newly snagged piece at the edge of the table, beside its previously nabbed mates.

He looked up at Mother Bridges.

Their eyes met.

For a moment, neither spoke.

At last, Mother Bridges sighed.

With one arm, she reached behind her back, her fingers probing for the bra strap's clasp.

CHAPTER
28

Technicians scurried here and there, plugged this into that, patched that into this, and fiddled with wires linking a cable to a junction box.

Just this side of apoplexy, the executive producer said, "Are you guys ever going to be ready?"

"We're ready," a technician sang out.

"He's ready to roll?" the producer asked Gerald Dorsett.

"Are you ready to roll?" Dorsett said into the telephone. He listened for a moment. "He says he's ready to roll."

"Tell him to roll," the producer said.

"Roll," Dorsett said into the phone.

In the converted double-wide that was Channel 34's control booth, Wilbur Morton set down the receiver, rubbed his sweaty palms together, and prayed a silent prayer.

Then he flipped a toggle on the jerry-rigged console.

The spools turned.

At network headquarters in New York City, in a chrome-and-glass tower looming over the Avenue of the Americas, black-and-white monitors came aglow with the snowy image of Police Officer Alvin Henderson's retreating posterior.

On the accompanying soundtrack was Morton's recorded voice. "Would it be the Buick dealer Dwight Bridges?"

The film ran out.

"That's it? That's the whole piece?" the executive news director asked.

"That's it? That's the whole piece?" Gerald Dorsett said into the telephone.

"It's as much as I could get," Wilbur Morton told him.

"It's as much as he could get," Dorsett told the New York crew.

For a moment, nobody said anything.

"So what?" a New York staffer said at last. "It's a coincidence, the whole thing. A crazy coincidence is all."

"Coincidence?" the news director asked. "Hoggzswallow Hollow? Dwight Bridges? And not just any Dwight Bridges, but a car dealer?"

"And not just a car dealer," said a technician from the back of the room, "but a Buick dealer."

"You think that's all a coincidence?" the news director asked.

"Okay, so it's some sort of hoax. A prank. An elaborate practical joke."

"Is there an atlas in this joint?" the director asked. "Anybody got an atlas? Somebody get me a motherfucking atlas."

"Somebody get him a motherfucking atlas," somebody said.

Somebody got him an atlas.

"Somebody open it to West Virginia."

Somebody opened it to West Virginia.

He pored over the map.

Sure enough, in microscopic typeface reserved for the smallest townships, tucked into the folds of the Larson Valley south of Wheeling, below Lewis Peak, approximately forty miles west of Charleston, there was a pale dot.

It could have been a printing error.

"Somebody get me a magnifying glass," the director said.

Somebody got him a magnifying glass.

Positioning the lens an inch above the map, he strained his eyes and barely made out the legend, in two-point font below the dot: *Hoggzswallow Hollow.*

In an instant, the crew was riding the elevator to the top floor, then climbing a ladder to a helipad on the roof, where a chopper awaited.

Its rotors were already in motion.

The crew boarded.

The party was aloft, putt-putting southward even before the reel of film, downstairs in the production offices, had rewound.

CHAPTER
29

Bridges awoke from a fitful nap as Air Force One descended bumpily into McCarran Airport. By this hour, the hills were a dusky desert purple, the sky a Crayola mélange of mango interlaced with notes of azure and teal.

A team of Secret Service personnel and Navy medics transferred a groggy Bridges from the plane to an awaiting limousine. With a phalanx of armored SUVs fore and aft, the limo departed the airport, then slid smoothly down the strip to the Desert Goliath Hotel, Country Club, Resort, Spa, and Casino.

"Running slick as shit." Buddy Scheib glanced at his watch as the entourage pulled up to the showroom's backstage entrance. "You made it with time to spare, Richie. Why, there are still two whole minutes to go before you're due onstage."

"Can't I go back to the suite first?" Bridges yawned. "I need to catch my breath, freshen up, put on my game face. I generally don't like to go on stage before taking a quick shower."

Bridges was struck by the irony of his remark.

Beyond the previous evening, he had no memory of ever hav-ing performed as a comedian. Yet here he was, expounding on his pre-performance protocols, as if he had pre-performance proto-cols, as if he were actually Richie Ritchie, comedic toast of the nation.

"A shower?" Buddy Scheib said, checking his Rolex. "Sure. Why not? How about also a shave?" After a pause, he said, "Might as well throw in a mani-pedi while we're at it, and a Brazilian bikini wax."

Except for the last item, none of that struck Bridges as a bad idea. He had heard of a mani-pedi, even if he had never actually had one, and was curious to try it out. He could not imagine, how-ever, what in the world might constitute a Brazilian bikini wax.

Between the present moment and the previous evening's performance, hadn't he visited Teheran, the Sinai Desert, and Washington, D.C., not to mention any number of parallel uni-verses and alternative eras?

Surely he was entitled to a break.

"We promised Avakian to have you on stage exactly per sched-ule," Scheib said. "As always, it's a full house. Every minute the customers spend in the showroom is a minute they're not in the casino. With wagering revenues averaging a million-eight per hour, a fifteen-minute delay costs management, let's see ..."

Scheib whipped out a pad and the much-chewed-upon stub of a pencil. He scratched, scribbled, scrawled. After some moments he gave up and said, "Well, a bunch of money."

He plopped the pencil and notepad back in his pocket.

"You pause to take a leak before you go onstage? It costs Avakian seventy-five, eighty grand. You fart, there's eight, maybe twelve hundred schmools right there. Hey, if the president hadn't lent you her plane, you'd have missed the gig entirely, and we'd be responsible for refunding the whole gate."

Bridges stretched his limbs.

He blinked his eyes.

"Freshen up in the dressing room," Scheib suggested. "Christ almighty, Rich, they call it a dressing room, but it's more like a goddamned luxury condo. In Burundi or Bhutan or wherever, there'd be twenty families living in it, and happy to do so, the envy of their shtetl, so to speak. Know what I'm talking?"

Bridges had no idea what he was talking.

"You'll prep in the dressing room. Splash some cold water on your face, put a damp rag on the back of your neck, whatever."

Scheib and the retinue of hangers-on hustled Bridges down the ramp. They led him through a pair of heavy steel doors that parted and closed automatically, and then through a maze of darkened corridors.

Soon enough, Bridges found himself slumped forward in a chair in the green room, facing the dressing-table mirror. Stationed behind him, Scheib maneuvered Bridges's arms into the sleeves of the maroon lamé tux.

In the background, the audience buzzed, and the band vamped.

Scheib could see that Bridges's energy was flagging. "Let's get a move on, Rich," he said, poking at the makeup pots on the table, then slapping pancake on Bridges's face.

"You all right?" he asked Bridges.

Bridges shrugged.

"Try to be just a tad upbeat tonight, Rich," Scheib said. "Your triumph in LA at that Holocaust gig earlier today got national exposure. As a result, there's gonna be live network coverage here tonight."

Knuckles rapped at the door. "Mr. Ritchie!" a voice called out. "You're on!"

"He's coming!" Scheib shouted at the door.

He turned back to Bridges. "Ready?"

"Ready?" Bridges yawned. "Yeah, sure I'm ready."

He heaved another heavy yawn.

"I'm ready for a nap. I'm ready for a year and a half of sweet, deep sleep."

"That's on tap," Scheib said, "right after this set. You're tired? When we're done here tonight, you decline the traditional post-performance pussy. You hop right into bed. Alone. You sleep all night, and all day if it suits you, right up until tomorrow's first set."

Scheib took a step back, assessing his client like a county tax auditor appraising a property. "By tomorrow night," he said, "you're fresh as a mother-jumping daisy, okay?"

"Mr. Ritchie?" the voice called out again from the hallway. "It's time! Time, Mr. Ritchie!"

"Here he comes!" the manager shouted at the door.

Scheib faced Bridges.

"Let's do it, Rich."

He thrust his hands under Bridges's arms and strained to hoist him upright.

Bridges resisted.

"Know what I could use?" Bridges said.

"What's that?"

"A little—what did you call it?—a little pick-me-up. An eye-opener."

"A little eye-opener?"

"That's what you called it," Bridges said. "Last night, just before I went on. You offered me a little eye-opener."

"A little eye-opener?"

"Is there an echo in here?" Bridges asked.

"I don't get what you're saying."

"That's what you called it," Bridges said.

In the background, the band shifted gears, segueing from a generic vamp to the full-blooded Richie Ritchie refrain. From outside the dressing room came the plea, "Mr. Ritchie! Your fanfare! You're on! Mr. Ritchie? Mr. Ritchie?"

"I told you he's coming!" Scheib hollered.

There was the thunder of rhythmic clapping.

"Rich! Eee! Rich! Eee!" the audience chanted.

"Sal-something," Bridges said to Scheib. "Premium something. Salvador something. Something like that. An eye-opener."

"Let's do it, Rich," Scheib pleaded, investing all of his strength into hauling Bridges to his feet.

Bridges remained seated.

"Not Salvador," Bridges now remembered. "Equestrian!" he said. "Door. Ian. That's it!"

"Door? Ian?" Scheib asked.

"Ecuadorian primo!" Bridges lit up like a magnesium road flare.

"You're talking lines? Snorts? Toots?" Scheib said. "Last night, with the back of your hand, you swept away the equivalent of the national budget of Azerbaijan. You don't remember? You squandered a whole oh-zee."

"Oh-zee?"

"Ounce."

Scheib reached into his jacket and withdrew a diminutive phial filled with white power. Affixed to it, secured by a delicate sterling chain, was a silver mini-spoon.

Scheib unscrewed the cap.

He dipped the spoon into the tiny bottle.

He withdrew a modest hill of powder.

He thrust it under Bridges's right nostril.

He said, "Now!"

Bridges snorted.

In an instant, his eyes popped wide open and flooded with tears.

Scheib extracted a second serving of the white dust. Positioning the spoon just below Bridges's left nostril, he said "Go!"

Bridges inhaled sharply.

He smiled serenely.

His body bobbed up and back where he sat, as if to offer an impression of Rabbi Shirley Shapiro davening.

Scheib said, "Now will you get your frigging butt on the frigging stage?"

Bridges arose from his chair and made his way to the dressing-room door.

Client and manager entered the corridor, where Boss Avakian stood waiting.

Navy-blue veins on Avakian's forehead, swollen to the caliber of garden hoses, throbbed in synch with his galloping pulse. "He's actually going to put in an appearance?" he inquired, his voice rancid with sarcasm. "Isn't that nice? The guy's gonna show his face to the customers. We are sincerely honored."

He offered Bridges a low, sweeping bow.

Closely following Scheib, Bridges made his way along the corridor to the wall of light. The cheering, stamping, and clapping grew more urgent.

Popping in and out of focus before the massive electronic light board, the shirt-sleeved technician waited. Avakian nodded to him. Shirtsleeves seized a telephone wired to the control panel on the wall. "Cue Richie's theme," he said into the receiver.

Next he snatched clusters of levers and attenuators, twisting, turning, toggling.

The wall of light fluctuated in intensity and hue.

The band stepped up the tempo to a sprint.

"Ladies and Gentlemen," the announcer's voice oozed like vapor from a thousand grates. "The fabulous Starshine Dome of the phenomenal Desert Goliath Hotel, Country Club, Resort, Spa, and Casino proudly presents … Richie Ritchie!"

The audience erupted like Vesuvius.

On the brink of his entrance, Bridges paused, took a deep breath, brushed back his hair, straightened his shoulders. A surge of energy rippled through him. He took a last look around at the army of backstage suck-ups.

Ultra-tight security was evident in the presence of a dozen uniformed security personnel. In the corner of his eye, Bridges noticed one particular guard, sweating and short of breath, as if just now having completed the Boston Marathon. There was something curious about the fellow, something eerily familiar. Bridges noticed that this particular officer sported a uniform that was different from the standard-issue Goliath starched tan and gray.

Now it all came into focus.

"Al!" Bridges said. "Al Henderson!"

Hoggzswallow Hollow police officer Alvin Henderson nodded in greeting.

Then, Henderson directed his gaze to the floor.

Pawing the ground, smiling awkwardly, he looked up again at Bridges.

Nodding and tipping his hat in acknowledgment, Henderson said, "Dwight."

CHAPTER
30

"Bedford Avenue, Duke!" the Shah of Iran hollered to Brooklyn Dodger centerfielder, cleanup hitter, and team captain Edwin Donald Snider.

Instead of putting one over the right field fence, however, where neighborhood kids were stationed in anticipation of copping a free ball, the batter dug for a low slider, grounding sharply to shortstop. Yankee Phil Rizzuto fielded the ball expertly as always. Pivoting, he tossed it to Moose Skowron at first, who caught it three full strides before Snider crossed the bag.

The field box seats had cost the quartet of fans twelve dollars, not each, but for the entire party, even including the post-season championship series surcharge of seventy-five cents per seat. Upon reassurance from the vendor that the dogs were Hebrew National and therefore pork-free, the Shah ordered for the group: one each for himself, Dwight Bridges, Dwight Bridges's mother, Henrietta, and Aahhotep Elouan.

The Egyptian astrophysicist's Israeli counterpart, theoretical mathematician Chaim Yitzkowitz, was nowhere to be seen.

"Seems like all the action is in New York City," the Shah said.

"What do you mean?" asked Mother Bridges.

"In the American League, there's no competition," he explained. "There's only the Yanks." He took a bite of his dog. "It's almost the same in the National League. The only serious rivalry is between two franchises, both of them in New York: the Dodgers and the Giants."

The Shah turned to Bridges. "Am I right?"

"Truth to tell," Bridges said. "I don't follow baseball. In fact, I don't follow sports at all." He took a bite of his own frank, and then asked the Shah, "How do you know so much about it?"

"We get the box scores in real time via a teletype feed at the Mirror Hall of the Sa'dabad complex of royal residences near Teheran," he said. "I've followed the Dodgers for as long as I can remember."

"But just last season," Aahhotep Elouan said, "neither the Yanks nor the Dodgers made it to the Series."

"All the same," the Shah said, "New York was represented, if merely by the Giants."

"But opposing the Giants," Mother Bridges said, "wasn't the Yankees but Cleveland."

"My mother follows the game more closely than I," Bridges said.

"Our mixed-breed Bedlington terrier, Corky, who died eleven years ago," Mother Bridges said, "follows the game more closely than you, Dwight."

"Last year was an aberration," the Shah said. "Cleveland was an anomaly. If you confuse the exception for the rule, you'll fall on your face every time."

Peering around at the decrepit cheese box of a ballpark that was Ebbets Field, with its rickety wooden bleachers and obstructed-view loge seats stationed directly behind steel support beams, the Egyptian said, "Sorry about all this. Apparently the tele-transporter continues to act up. It has somehow delivered us to Flatbush in the autumn of 1955."

"If the contraption is going to take us to a mistaken destination in time and place," the Shah said, "let it be the 1955 World Series."

Looking around at fans seated in adjacent boxes, he beckoned his companions to lean in close.

His voice dropped to a whisper, and he shielded his mouth with one hand. "I don't want to spoil the fun for the rest of the crowd," he said under his breath. "This is merely the opener. The series will go the limit, so they still have to get through six more games. We know from our experience with the transporter, however, that this is the only season throughout the franchise's entire Brooklyn tenure that the Dodgers win the Series."

"I don't really care that much for the game," Aahhotep said. "Frankly, I could never quite follow the rules."

"They're complicated," the Shah said. "I've never understood why, for example, it's three strikes and four balls instead of the other way around."

"We have designated the baseball seasons," Aahhotep continued, "as benchmarks to gauge the transporter's era-shifting. It appears the data may have migrated from the power-management circuits into the central processor, thereby corrupting the hyper-text-markup protocols."

"I see," Bridges said, as if he had the even the humblest understanding of what had been said.

"It could explain how we ended up here?" the Shah asked Aahhotep.

She nodded.

The Shah looked around at his companions, then surveyed the broader body of fans throughout the park. In a low voice, he said to the group, "Just wait till you see what Jackie Robinson does here today in the ninth."

CHAPTER
31

The network helicopter hovered high above the slag heaps and deforested mountain slopes that deprived Hoggzswallow Hollow of television reception. As the aircraft descended through the fog, the township's grid of streets came into focus, indicating civilization, or what passed for civilization, in this lost corner of the American heartland.

Hollering to be heard above the rotors, the pilot asked the executive news director, "Where do you want me to put it?"

The director was tempted to tell him.

Instead, he jammed a set of Bausch and Lomb binoculars in front of his face.

"Can anybody spot the station?" Gerald Dorsett called out, scanning the landscape in search of a transmission tower, a satellite dish, an uplink, downlink, any old link.

"There!" the director said, pointing downward.

"Where?" the pilot asked. "I don't see any TV station."

"Forget the TV station," the director said. "I'm indicating that car lot."

"Car lot?"

"Auto dealership," he said. "Hang on a moment. Let me look again." He lowered the field glasses to his chest, twirled the focus knob, then repositioned the lenses once again before his face.

He rotated the knob a tad forward, then two tads back.

After a moment, he said, "Buicks."

The chopper maintained its lumbering descent.

Slowly, the oversize eggbeater settled onto the asphalt fronting the darkened Bridges Buick showroom, coming to rest between a coal-gray Regal sedan and a two-tone Century coupe.

"Nobody's here," Gerald Dorsett said.

"You think?" the director said with a note of scorn.

"Whether or not anyone's here is of no consequence," Dorsett said. Splaying the inverted thumbs and forefingers of both hands, positioning them opposite one another, he constructed in the air a rectangular frame. Now, doing his impression of Cecil B. DeMille, he panned across the lot, settling at last upon the Bridges Buick sign.

"If this is all we get," he said, "it's a scoop of colossal proportion."

He turned to his team. "Roll film."

Audio and video equipment strapped to their bodies, the crew leaped from the aircraft and commenced raking the dealership with footage.

"What are we shooting?" a member of the crew asked. "There's nothing happening."

The cameras continued to crank.

"Irregardless," the director said, "we're smack-dab in front of Bridges Buick in Hoggzswallow Hollow, West Virginia. That's no small thing."

"*Regardless,*" Dorsett said, "or *irrespective.* There's no such word as *irregardless.*"

"Really?" the director said. "Is there such a word as *go-fuck-yourself?*"

He turned to the cameraman. "Make sure you get a close-up of that *Dwight Bridges, Proprietor* sign."

"Where do you want me for my standup, my on-camera commentary?" Gerald Dorsett asked.

The director stared a hole through Dorsett's head.

"You prefer instead just a voice-over?" Dorsett asked. "That it? You think an off-screen narration would suffice?"

"What would suffice," the director said, pointing to the far end of the lot, "would be for you to deliver your ass to that phone booth yonder."

In the era at hand, payphones had not yet gone extinct.

"Check the directory," he continued, "and get me the address for the TV station. See if there's a listing for Dwight Bridges's residence."

Dorsett performed as instructed.

Soon enough, the helicopter was again airborne. It drifted above Deerfield, and now Old Deerfield.

It touched down at last in Bridges's front yard.

"Keep them blades cranking," the director commanded the pilot.

He stepped from the helicopter, approached the house, climbed the stairs to the porch, and rapped on the door. "Dwight Bridges?" he called out. "Hello? Anybody home?"

There was only silence.

After a decent interval, the director stepped back. He barked at his crew, "Let's roll!"

The team departed the chopper.

They assembled on Dwight Bridges's lawn. They circumnavigated the house, filming it from every angle.

At last, they returned to the helicopter.

The director settled into his jump seat behind the pilot. Securing his safety harness, he ordered the captain as one might a cabbie or, in a subsequent era, an Uber driver: "Police headquarters." Turning toward his team, the director said, "Let's scare up this fellow, what'd they call him?"

Referring to his notepad, Gerald Dorsett said, "Police Officer Alvin Henderson."

"That's the guy," the director said.

The chopper wafted skyward.

Within minutes, it sank once again to an altitude only several feet above the ground. It hovered there, opposite the shabby Coolidge-era structure that served as the township's police headquarters.

Below, walking up the path, shouting to be heard above the rotors, was a short, stocky fireplug of a fellow, a bushy-bearded man in his mid-twenties. His scruffy whiskers made it possible to mistake him for someone more mature. With one hand, he steadied his knit skullcap, which threatened at any moment to be blown away by the rotors' wash.

"Pardon me, gentlemen," Chaim Yitzkowitz said in his hummus-and-tahini laced Middle Eastern drawl, "but what's all the excitement?"

CHAPTER
32

Not at Ebbets Field but Yankee Stadium, the ninth inning of the seventh game was just getting underway.

Aahhotep Elouan and Dwight Bridges, propped up against the headboard of the king bed in their Delta SKY 360 Luxury Suite, struggled mightily to catch their breath.

Overlooking the infield from high above the visitor's dugout, the unit was a virtual penthouse. Through the mirrored floor-to-ceiling one-way window, Yankee left fielder Elston Howard—the franchise's first player of color—could be seen standing in the batter's box facing Dodgers pitching ace Johnny Podres.

Aahhotep threw back the covers, climbed out of the bed, and retrieved her lavender silk drawers from the floor where Bridges had flung them sometime during the bottom of the sixth. Scattered about the chamber was the wreckage of the dinner the couple had consumed, delivered earlier by white-coated servers bearing trays of sterling silver. The munchies had included an eclectic array of appetizers, among them Coquilles St. Jacques, Mediterranean saffron shrimp kabobs, pheasant salad puffs, balsamic-glazed ahi rolls, and tomato buffalo caprese.

It was a tasting menu half a century before anybody had heard of tasting menus.

"Whatever happened to 'peanuts and Cracker Jack'?" Bridges asked.

There was also a bottle of Chateau d'Esclans Garrus Rose 1948, and two Saint Louis Crystal Thistle Gold Waterford glasses. As Bridges refilled the twin flutes, Aahhotep asked, "Whatever happened to Schaefer beer?"

One foot at a time, pointing her toes like a prima ballerina donning Capezios, the astrophysicist stepped into her undies. Now, settling her butt at the edge of the bed, she pulled on her hose.

"Whatever happened to commercial jingles?" Bridges asked.

Aahhotep sang, "Schaefer. Is the. One beer to have ..."

Bridges crooned in response, "When you're. Having. More than. One."

Aahhotep sang, "My beer. Is Rheingold. The dry beer ..."

Bridges sang, "Think of Rheingold. Whenever. You buy beer ..."

"Whatever happened to the 'house that Ruth built?'" Aahhotep asked, "The original Yankee Stadium?" She liberated her bra from the tangle of clothing on the floor, watching Bridges watching her as she hooked the clasps, threaded her arms through the straps, and pulled the garment over her head and shoulders, kneading her ample breasts like cookie dough as she molded them into the cups.

"Once again, we can thank the holographic tele-transporter's dicey digital navigation protocols," the Egyptian astrophysicist said. "Not only has it taken us to the World Series in a ballpark that won't even be built for forty years, but the '55 Series opening and closing games were played not here in Bronx but at Ebbets Field in the Brooklyn."

"Not *Bronx*," Bridges corrected her. "*The Bronx*."

"The Bronx," Aahhotep said.

"And not *the Brooklyn*," Bridges said. "Simply *Brooklyn*."

"Brooklyn," she said.

After a moment, Bridges said, "I thought you didn't follow baseball."

"Google."

"Google?"

"It's something I encountered in yet another misdirected tele-transporter journey to an alternative era. When its day comes, Google will be like of one of those ancient, all-knowing oracles from the age of the pharaohs," she said, "except that it won't be ancient, and it won't be an oracle."

"I see," Bridges said, nodding.

He was getting used to saying "I see" in response to propositions that he did not see.

"Instead of an oracle," the Egyptian continued, "it will be an algorithm."

"I see," Bridges said.

He stepped out of the bed and fetched his own apparel, which lay sprawled across an Ottoman where the garments had been abandoned midst the seventh-inning stretch. "You mean during the first game," he asked, "when Robinson stole home in the last of the ninth, that actually happened not here but at Ebbets Field?"

"Depends what you mean by *actually*."

"And catcher Yogi Berra's quarrel with home-plate umpire Augie Donatelli disputing the call?" Bridges asked. "That all took place not in the Bronx but Brooklyn?"

Aahhotep nodded. "That's how Wikipedia will tell it someday, in a parallel universe," she said, "during an alternative millennium."

Bridges nodded and said, "I see."

He did not ask her to translate *Wikipedia*.

As she slid her arms through the sleeves of her floral-eyelet-embroidered crop top, she said, "For a fellow who knows nothing about baseball, you seem to have picked up a lot of the lingo."

"I'm a quick read," Bridges said.

As the two continued dressing, pitcher Johnny Podres went into his trademark whirlybird windup.

Yankee batter Howard cocked his bat and awaited the arrival of the cross-stitched sphere.

CHAPTER
33

Dorsett and his crew dropped to the tarmac from the chopper, which maintained its position, hovering only a couple of feet above the ground.

The squad approached the entrance to police headquarters.

The door opened and Deputy Ernest J. Saunders, stretching and yawning, stepped outside without his jacket, hunching his shoulders against the November chill.

"Officer Alvin Henderson?" the director asked Saunders.

"He's not," Chaim Yitzkowitz said.

"He's not what?" Dorsett said.

"He's not Henderson."

"Oh," Dorsett said. "And who are you?"

"I'm Dr. Chaim Yitzkowitz."

"Oh" was all Saunders could think of to say.

"I'm a theoretical mathematician. I've come here from an alternative era and parallel dimension."

"Right," Saunders said, nodding. "Got it."

"This guy is not Alvin Henderson," Yitzkowitz said. "I'm looking for him myself. My journey through the space/time continuum enables me to identify a number of the personnel in the presently unfolding narrative."

Everybody took a moment to digest the information.

"I would recognize not only Henderson and Dwight Bridges, but even Dwight's mother, Henrietta," he said, "whom I first encountered prior to her tryst with the Shah."

"Tryst with the Shah," the deputy said, nodding.

"The Shah of Iran," Yitzkowitz said.

The others now joined the deputy in nodding.

Yitzkowitz continued, "I'm eager to track down this fellow, this law-enforcement officer, this Henderson."

"So am I," Deputy Saunders said. "Al's gone off somewhere. Must be some fair distance, because he's way overdue to relieve me. Frankly, I'm concerned. It's not like Al to take off without a word. Why do you need to find him?"

"We wanted to interview him," Dorsett said.

"Not you," Saunders said. "I was talking to Mr. Yitzko-whatever."

"... witz," Chaim said.

"You arrive in a big, noisy chopper," Saunders said to Dorsett. "You got a cadre of high-priced techno personnel with you, so I figure you're important. Still, here in Hoggzswallow Hollow, we're mired in old-fashioned notions like backwoods decency, dignity, courtesy, home-fried country-style manners, all that traditional honey-drenched Southern sentiment."

He turned back to Chaim. "Now, Mr. Witz ..."

"Yitz ..."

"Mr. Yitz ..."

"Yitzkowitz."

"Yitzkowitz. Did I get that right?"

Chaim nodded.

"What was it I could help you with, Mr. Yitzkowitz?"

"Dr. Yitzkowitz."

"Do you have any intel regarding Dwight Bridges or his mom?" Dorsett said, jumping in. "You say the woman's name is Bridges?"

"Didn't I tell you something about backwoods decency?" Deputy Saunders said.

"We're looking for a Bridges," Dorsett said. "Dwight Bridges, to be precise."

"So am I," the Israeli scientist said, "to be precise."

Everyone's attention was now disrupted by squealing brakes as the Channel Six newsmobile skidded to a stop in front of the police station, inscribing upon the pavement four dark arcs, like oversized commas drafted in burnt rubber.

The driver's door flew open with the engine idling.

Wilbur Morton hit the ground running, his camera bouncing on his shoulder, its movement cranking, its film rolling. Peering through the lens, he recorded the chopper, the network crew, the Israeli theoretical mathematician Dr. Chaim Yitzkowitz, and Deputy Saunders, all the while peppering them with questions. "What's the story? What's with the network helicopter?"

"Who're you?" Gerald Dorsett asked him.

"That's Wilbur Morton," Chaim Yitzkowitz explained, "your local TV anchor. News, sports, weather, commercials, whatever."

"Mr. Yitzkowitz," Wilbur asked. "Do I have that right?

"Dr. Yitzkowitz," Chaim said.

"Have you seen Dwight?"

"Everybody and his brother," Chaim Yitzkowitz said, "apparently even his own mother, seems to be looking for Dwight."

"Mr. Morton," the news director began, "may I ask you a question?" Wilbur Morton pried his eye from the lens.

"No time to talk just now," Morton said. "We stand at the preci-
pice of an historic event right here in Hoggzswallow Hollow. I just
now motored past the cable crew on the highway. They're about
to graft the last splice. It's like driving the golden spike into the
final tie of the transcontinental railway a hundred years ago or
whenever, in Utah, or wherever. Hoggzswallow Hollow's about to
enter the twentieth century. Starting this very night, there's gonna
be multiple channels airing episodes of *Get Smart, Gilligan's Island,
Gomer Pyle.*"

After a moment he added, "And those are just the Gs."

"Could we ask you just one question?" Gerald Dorsett said.

"Absolutely yes, but first I gotta get to the station, throw the
switch. We can talk over there."

With his Auricon CineVoice 16mm sound-on-film camera still
riding his shoulder, a tangled train of wires trailing him, Wilbur
Morton scrambled into the newsmobile. He settled behind the
wheel. Reaching over the equipment stacked in his lap, he seized
the floor-mount lever and dropped the engine into gear.

The car lurched backward.

Executing a three-point turn, Morton steered the vehicle down
the street.

The camera crew clambered aboard the helicopter.

The news director instructed the pilot, "Follow that car!"

A minute later, the chopper again drifted low over Hoggzswallow
Hollow, stalking the Channel Six newsmobile, arriving finally at
the broadcast facility's ramshackle excuse for a command center.

CHAPTER
34

The Brooklyn Dodgers were the workingman's team.

Their trademark blue uniforms matched their fans' collars.

The club's name was derived from the population in Flatbush known as "trolley dodgers," laborers who commuted to their jobs via public transportation, occasionally having to leap out of the way of oncoming trams.

Yankee pinstripes, on the other hand, reflected the upscale attire, the tweed suits and button-down white collars worn to the office by the team's own fans. The New York club embodied capitalist, conglomerate, colonialist, corporatist culture. And those were just the Cs.

Executives traveled to the ballpark not in trolleys but Chrysler Fifth Avenues, Chrysler Newports, and Chrysler New Yorkers.

And those were just the Chryslers.

Elston Howard made his way from the Yankee dugout to the rack. He withdrew his Rawlings Adirondack ash bat from the available weaponry. He moved over to the on-deck circle, where he took a couple of trial swings while waiting for Moose Skowron to finish his turn at the plate.

Thousands of fans directed their attention to the action on the field. They had no reason to notice the woman clad in a charcoal head-to-toe burka, including full veil, making her way up the stairs from the field boxes rising above the third baseline. Ascending to the Delta 360 Luxury Skye Suites level, she carried a long, narrow canvas bag that could have been designed to accommodate a billiards cue.

In the suite atop the stands, Mother Bridges extricated herself from the tangle of sheets scattered across the mattress. The chaos of linens offered stark testimony to the robust nature of the recent dalliance.

She slipped quietly from the bed to the floor.

From the bedspread and linens strewn about the carpet, she retrieved her underwear.

She stepped into the bloomers, pulled them up, and climbed back onto the bed beside the Shah, who had drifted off into the most preternaturally restful post-coital slumber in the history of erotic aftermath.

She settled her body comfortably against the monarch's back.

His eyes popped open.

He rotated his body to face his partner.

He put his arms around her.

Their mouths met.

They swapped a barrel of saliva.

Their lips finally came apart with a moist pop.

Henrietta Bridges asked the Shah, "Do you really think I'm hot?"

"I do," he said.

"But I'm a gray-haired bag of bones."

"The womanly bones of a womanly woman," the Shah said.

They lay there together, spooning, stretching, and yawning.

"Regarding your hair," the Shah continued, "you would be surprised how many men view gray hair as seductive, particularly on a mature woman who remains fit. There is something about a gentlewoman who has the courage to let her tresses go silver that men find sensual."

They repositioned their bodies on the bed. Facing each other, they embraced like lovers sculpted by Rodin.

The door to the suite flew open.

The couple looked up from their clutch.

The former Queen of Persia, Soraya Esfandiary-Bakhtiary, one among the Shah's previous wives—perhaps the third, at most the fourth—stepped through the door.

She tossed back her headscarf.

"Soraya!" the Shah said.

"Reza!" the woman said.

For a moment, no one said anything at all.

Then the Shah said, "Don't get the wrong idea."

The intruder spoke again.

"You miserable, lying, cheating, faithless, philandering, adulterous piece of Persian shit."

She set down the long canvas tote at the foot of the bed.

She unzipped its zipper.

From the bag she withdrew a Remington Model 870 Express Super Magnum hardwood pump-action shotgun.

CHAPTER
35

Inside, the network crew crowded together before the spit-and-baling-wire control console, shoulder to shoulder with Wilbur Morton.

On a nine-inch black-and-white monitor there unfolded the hundred-and-forty-seventh airing of the 1958 Vincent Price movie, *The Fly*, one of the half-dozen pictures—spliced, re-spliced, and re-re-spliced—constituting Channel 34's film library. The tattered 16mm print was threaded onto a primitive video film chain as a repeating loop. It required, therefore, no projectionist to rewind, change reels, ride focus, or manage any other task.

Wilbur yanked a lever, shutting down the projector.

The video image went to a fuzzy gray.

He seized another switch.

He inhaled a deep breath, then let it out.

He announced to the group, "Here goes."

He flicked the switch.

Nothing happened.

Now, abruptly, the gray screen went to nonsense white, an anarchic arrangement of visual static that looked like the crowd at a baseball game viewed from a satellite in outer space, a seething, bubbling, pulsing, frothy off-white. It was accompanied, appropriately, by white sound: a hissing, schussing, formless, ethereal, electronic whisper.

Despair settled over Wilbur Morton like a shroud.

"Appears they haven't hooked it up just yet," he said. "I drove past the cable-laying road crew not ten minutes ago, all of them on overtime. They were braiding the final coaxial splice. The foreman told me we'd be connected momentarily."

For a moment, no one said a word.

Finally, the news director inquired delicately, "We had some questions about your network feed earlier this afternoon. We were curious to ask you—"

At that precise moment, the monitor's image rippled, fluttered, flickered.

It came alive with a coherent image.

It was a commercial for Schaefer beer.

Wilbur Morton grew dizzy with excitement. "Do you see that? Do you? Do you see that?" He shook his head in awe. "That's the CBS affiliate out of Richmond!"

He flicked a switch.

There appeared the gameshow *Dollar a Second*, hosted by Jan Murray.

He flicked it again. There was local news from Charleston, West Virginia, covering a Girl Scouts bake sale at a church parking lot.

He flicked it again. There was an agricultural report from Charleston, North Carolina, featuring soy beans and tobacco.

He flicked it again.

The same Schaeffer beer spot, but this time out of Pensacola.

"A miracle of God," Morton swooned.

He flicked the switch.

The tube lit up with the latest *Munsters* episode.

He flicked it once more.

There was a continuous readout of temperature, humidity, barometric pressure, and wind velocity from the naval weather station atop Mount Carrol at Eagle Bluff, Kentucky. "This is positively astonishing. Can you believe it? Can you?"

All the while, in the background, outside the shabby studio, there was the sound of the network helicopter hovering, its prop wash bending the trees, kicking up a tempest of pebbles, dust, and leaves.

Wilbur flicked the switch again.

On screen there materialized the image of an audience in a packed nightclub. The telecast originated live and direct, as the announcer informed the viewers, from the fabulous Starshine Dome of the phenomenal Desert Goliath Hotel, Country Club, Resort, Spa, and Casino in Las Vegas, Nevada.

CHAPTER
36

The Harley Roadster 900 growled its way along Guatemala's sinuous Route 40, a couple of hours south of the Mexican state of Chiapas, perhaps sixty miles east of Quetzaltenango. Arriving at the intersection of Highway 2, the bike slowed, then came to a halt, its brushed-nickel Predator 6.5-horsepower engine idling at roadside.

Swathed head to toe in black leather and wearing a Biltwell custom helmet completely obscuring his face, the rider dismounted. He raised the headgear's tinted Plexiglas shield and withdrew a map from the saddlebag. He studied the map for a moment, then returned it to the bag.

Regarding the crossroad, the rider thought of Yankees catcher Yogi Berra. Legendary for his malapropisms, Berra had once declared, "When you come to a fork in the road, take it."

The rider climbed back onto his bike, dropped it into gear, and veered left onto the intersecting byway.

He rode now for an hour before turning onto yet another road, this one unidentified by signage. Except for loose gravel, the route was unpaved. A short while later, he transited to a still more primitive path, a rutted dirt trail snaking its way through the underbrush of the tropical rain forest whose canopy of mahogany, kapok, and acai cast a shadow as dark as night.

At long last, he arrived at a clearing dominated by a thatched hut and corrugated steel shed. He killed the engine, dismounted, and made his way toward the crude dwelling.

As he approached the structure, the door swung open.

A lowland gorilla shambled out.

Upon encountering each other, man and ape froze in place.

Simian and rider stared long and hard into each other's eyes.

Now the animal waved his arms this way and that, bending his elbows, gesturing energetically with his fingers and hands in the manner of American Sign Language.

The motorcyclist responded with similar such moves.

Speaking aloud, the ape said, "Ba'ax ka wa'alik."

"Ma'lob chi'inil K'iin" the rider said, nodding and bowing. "I'm pleased to meet you."

"Me llamo Bongo," the gorilla said. "Mucho gusto en conocerte."

The monkey's Spanish was infused with notes of Castellano, the lilting inflection causing him to sound like a standup comedian doing an impression of Ricardo Montalbán.

"Sorry?" the rider said. "I didn't quite get that. My Yucatec Maya is stronger than my high school Spanish."

"I'n k'aaba Bongo," the monkey said. "My name is Bongo. I'm pleased to meet you."

"She taught you to speak?" the rider said.

"I taught her to listen," Bongo said.

The rider shook his head in wonder and awe. Here was a low-land gorilla who could not only speak like a human, but in multiple languages. Now the ape said, "She's waiting for you."

"Gracias," the rider responded.

He did not know a whole lot more Spanish than that.

Seizing a machete leaning against the shed, the gorilla said, "Sígueme, por favor. Please follow me."

Bongo and his guest departed the clearing and traipsed through the forest with the monkey in the lead, cutting vines and hacking away at bamboo with the razor-sharp blade.

Eventually they came upon an imposing mound overgrown with brush and rubber trees. Rising more than a hundred feet above the floodplain, the formation was so obscured by vegetation that only a seasoned explorer would have recognized it for what it was: a pre-Columbian indigenous monolith.

The motorcyclist followed Bongo up the pyramid's north face.

The steps were so narrow as to require the climbers to zigzag their way to the top, slithering like serpents.

At the pinnacle, there was a narrow entryway.

From his jacket, the rider withdrew a HaloXT tactical flashlight. Peering down into the interior, he projected a xenon-fueled beam that was as bright as a Klieg raking the sky at a Hollywood premiere.

The gorilla led the rider down a wooden ladder, deep into the structure's bowels. The pair landed at the bottom of a stone chamber whose walls were crisscrossed with row upon row of cryptic glyphs featuring images of what appeared to be intertwined asps, the same breed of snake carved into the Egyptian pyramids thousands of years ago, thousands of miles across the globe.

At center stood some sort of machine, approximately the size of a Volkswagen Beetle. The device rested on a platform with built-in rotors, rollers, and wheels apparently designed to enable it to revolve, rotate, adjust, position, and reposition itself.

As the motorcyclist regarded the device, a trapdoor in the chamber's dirt floor swung up and open.

A woman clad in overalls, wearing a tool belt and wielding a heavy-gauge hex wrench, stepped into the chamber, letting the hatch fall closed below her. "Welcome," she said.

The visitor continued to stare at the apparatus.

"Never seen one of these?" she asked.

Her guest shook his head.

"It's a positron-emission muon ionic holographic tele-transporter," said former U.S. president Sarah Palin.

CHAPTER
37

The camera tracked Richie Ritchie strolling from the show-room's wings to center stage.

The audience roared so loudly, Wilbur Morton worried the audio console would blow a circuit. Bridges smiled and waved, waved and smiled. After a period lasting as long as the Iron Age, the tumult subsided to a murmur.

"Thank you so much," Dwight Bridges said to the packed venue. "God bless each and every one of you. You people are beautiful. I mean it. I really do. I really, truly mean it."

Here he paused, marinating in the audience's exaltation.

"I've said it before and I'll say it again," Bridges continued once the room had settled down. "I haven't a clue as to how I come to be here tonight. Or last night. Or any night. I've told you before, and I'll tell you again, as far as I know, my name is Dwight Bridges, and I'm a Buick dealer from Hoggzswallow Hollow, West Virginia."

As always, the crowd rose to its feet, chanting Bridges's lines along with him as he spoke them, then erupting yet again into a firestorm of approval.

Basking in the ovation, he did not notice a uniformed police officer emerging from the wings, tentatively making his way toward center stage, finally positioning himself just behind Bridges.

Wallowing shamelessly in the audience's adulation, Bridges continued nodding and smiling. Was he actually beginning to enjoy the benefits that stardom, however inexplicably, had bestowed upon him?

"Dwight?" Henderson inquired.

Bridges turned.

"Al!" he said. "What in the world are you doing here?"

Before Henderson could respond, Bridges turned to the audience.

Somewhat bemused, which is to say wholly in keeping with his trademark deadpan persona, Bridges announced, "Folks, please welcome Hoggzswallow Hollow police officer Alvin Henderson."

Cheers swelled; applause grew to a frenzy.

Not knowing what else to do, Henderson offered an embarrassed half smile, then waved his hand in feeble greeting.

As if it were all but a single word—indeed a single syllable—Henderson leaned forward and muttered into the microphone, sounding like one of the Strip's plentiful Elvis impersonators, "Thang-ya-verra-mush."

The audience went wild.

After what felt like a week or two, the commotion ebbed to a muffled rumble.

Bridges asked Henderson, "Al? What brings you here tonight?"

Henderson said. "I'm placing you under arrest."

The audience screamed with laughter; the room shook with upheaval bordering on anarchy.

"Is that a fact?"

"You have the right to remain silent," Henderson said. "In the event you choose to speak," he continued, "anything you say can and will be used against you in a court of law."

The audience rose to its feet, laughing, tears streaming down their faces.

They yelled and hollered and howled their appreciation, their affection, their respect, their love, their lust, their passion, their straight-ahead, flat-out, all-in, all-out awe.

CHAPTER
38

The rider scanned the fanciful creation with his high-tech flashlight.

Its beam glinted off the surface of the holographic tele-transporter and, surrounding it in the darkness, a series of translucent interlocking baseball diamonds.

Each infield permeated another on multiple planes, floating like clouds. Each had its own home plate, bases, pitcher's mound, plus a webbed outfield stretching the length and breadth of the enclosure.

Now the tele-transporter apparatus commenced to tremble.

It emitted a subtle hum.

Its surface came aglow, radiating a phosphorescent sheen.

A panel slid open.

Out stepped Aahhotep Elouan and Chaim Yitzkowitz.

The Israeli withdrew a handkerchief from his pocket and mopped his brow. Regarding the rider, he said, "It's kind of warm in here, wouldn't you say? Aren't you hot?"

The motorcyclist set down his flashlight, slipped off his leather jacket, and removed the helmet.

Bongo the gorilla asked the rider, "Bix a k' a'aba?"

"What'd he say?" asked Aahhotep.

"I know Hebrew and English," Chaim said, "some Arabic and also some Yiddish. My Yucatec Maya, however, is a little rusty."

"I'm asking him his name," the lowland gorilla explained in unaccented English. The rider said to Bongo, "I'n k'aaaba'e Buddy Scheib."

"You speak the Maya language?" Sarah Palin asked.

"I've studied Xinca, an indigenous Guatemalan language," Buddy Scheib said, "and Garifuna, a parochial Arawakan tongue still spoken in some regions by descendants of pre-historical tribes along the Caribbean coast. The vocabularies and syntax are close enough so that if you know a little Q'anjob'al, you can fake your way through a host of Yucatecan dialects."

Sarah Palin gestured broadly with both arms, indicating the array of baseball universes. "Since resigning my office and splitting the toxic DC beltway scene a year or so ago, and spending several months here," she said, "I've been trying to decipher the meaning of all this."

Chaim asked, "Does everything have to have meaning?"

"Chaim and I have discovered over our years working together," Aahhotep Elouan said, "that there are phenomena in this world that are beyond understanding."

"There are actions and circumstances," the Israeli said, "that cannot be explained."

"As Yogi Berra famously put it," Aahhotep said, "sometimes a cigar is just a cigar."

"Was that Yogi Berra?" Bongo the gorilla asked. "I thought it was Freud."

"Freud?" Chaim said. "What team did he play for?"

"The Yankees," Buddy Scheib said. "A pitcher. Whitey Freud."

"Not Freud," the ape said. "Ford. Whitey Ford. A southpaw celebrated for his slider."

"I'm glad we got that straightened out," Sarah Palin said. "My question stands, however." Once again indicating the multitude of interlacing baseball diamonds suspended in the ether, she said, "What the eff is this all about?"

"Eternal life," said Buddy Scheib.

"That's what the pharaohs sought," Egyptian Aahhotep said. "That's what all of history's embalmed totalitarians coveted, from Tutankhamun, to Stalin, to Mao, to Trump."

"Trump?" Buddy Scheib asked.

"A TV emcee," the gorilla said, "hosting a reality show. In a parallel time and alternate universe, he is elected to public office."

"Not exactly elected," Aahhotep said.

"An actor who goes into politics?" Buddy Scheib asked. "You mean Ronald Reagan."

"No," Bongo the lowland gorilla said. "Reagan hosted *General Electric Theater* half a century earlier. That wasn't a reality show. It was anthology drama."

"An actor is elected president of the United States?" Aahhotep said.

"That shouldn't be a surprise," Sarah Palin said. "My fifteen-minute career in public service taught me that while some actors are politicians, all politicians are actors. The first actor elected president was George Washington."

"The guy I'm talking about," Aahhotep said, "worked also as a Manhattan realtor."

She pronounced it *reel-litter.*

"And after his term, like Stalin and Mao and the pharaohs, he was embalmed?" asked Sarah Palin.

"Not after but before. He is the first president to serve while embalmed."

"Been there, done that," Sarah Palin said. "Sure, there's great medical coverage, including dental, and there's an indoor pool, but otherwise it's nothing but heartache, frustration, and grief."

"A real estate agent as president of the United States?" Buddy Scheib said. "Sounds like material from a Richie Ritchie monologue."

He turned to Sarah Palin.

"You've been searching in the wrong direction," he told her. "You've been looking toward the beginning, but the answer is at the end. The end is the beginning."

"Of course," Bongo said, rolling his eyes. "That explains it."

Here was a lowland gorilla who could not only speak several languages but also traffic in sarcasm. Here was a primate who was smart enough to understand that there were things he was not smart enough to understand.

"I still don't get it," Sarah Palin said.

"Space is curved," Buddy Scheib said. "Hit a homerun far enough, and it'll land in foul territory. Hit a foul ball far enough, it lands fair. The same location in the universe is fair or foul, depending upon who's looking."

"And where they're standing," Chaim said.

"And the route taken to get there," Aahhotep said.

"And the time of day," Chaim said.

"Or night," Buddy Scheib said.

A glimmer of enlightenment settled over Sarah Palin. "You're talking about relativity," she said.

"And topology," Bongo said, "the mathematics of surfaces."

"Precisely," Buddy Scheib said.

"Now do you get it?" Aahhotep Elouan asked.

"I do," Sarah Palin said, slowly nodding. "The answer's been right before my eyes since I was six years old and my daddy took me to see the Sitka Oilers whip the Ketchikan Glacier Pilots in my first baseball game."

She paused to let it all sink in.

Buddy Scheib said, "Fair is foul and foul is fair."

"Yogi Berra?" Chaim Yitzkowitz asked.

"Shakespeare," Buddy Scheib said.

"*Macbeth*," Bongo the lowland gorilla said.

CHAPTER
39

I t was a big day for breaks.

The courthouse sketch artists, for instance, those fellows who scratch out drawings of the goings-on inside court, they don't work every day of the week, fifty-two weeks a year. They work when there's work, and there's work whenever a judge bans media from a trial.

Regarding the action presently before the court, the judge had prohibited cameras, lights, cables, and all manner of broadcast paraphernalia—hence, the army of sketch guys. Outside, however, on the front steps and spilling into the street were all kinds of media: print, radio, TV. High-tech trucks lofted satellite dishes to their maximum height, combing the heavens for the ghost of a signal.

Beyond the circus of reporters surrounding the courthouse were thousands of Richie Ritchie fans, some local, others from out of state. There was also a substantial international contingent who had traveled from places as distant as Burkina Faso, and Sri Lanka when it was still called Ceylon.

It was a scene straight out of that late '40s black-and-white Kirk Douglas movie about a man stuck in a mineshaft. The film was based upon television's inaugural media frenzy, a true-to-life drama that had unfolded in Southern California in 1948, when three-year-old Kathy Fiscus perished after spending several days trapped in an abandoned well. Bridges and his mother had once viewed a blurry print of the movie on Hoggzswallow Hollow's Channel 34.

Newsmen dispatched to Hoggzswallow Hollow for the trial—in those days there were precious few newswomen—presented their standups on camera and off. There were voice-overs, commentary, color, analysis. With the governor having called up the National Guard, there were also squadrons of uniformed law-enforcement personnel.

Neither Gerald Dorsett nor Wilbur Morton, however, could cop even the semblance of a break.

Dorsett was nowhere in sight but, instead, back in New York at the network's offices on Sixth Avenue, once again fetching coffee for people more important than himself.

And Wilbur Morton? No sooner had cable penetrated Hoggzswallow Hollow than he was busted to Weather and banished to a station in the desert Southwest, a region that had no weather.

Within an hour of being escorted back to Hoggzswallow Hollow by Officer Alvin Henderson, Richie Ritchie was booked, arraigned, and released on his own recognizance. Back home, emerging from the shower, he found himself once again to be bald.

With the story morphing into tabloid fodder across the globe, and attention mounting over the felony vandalism trial about to commence, a car purchased from Bridges Buick had become an international trophy. Everybody wanted one. To handle the crush,

Bridges hired a dozen salesmen, who doled out vehicles like papal indulgences. Interested parties were required to fill out a lengthy application including a "statement of purpose" to be evaluated by a committee of dealership personnel. Preferences were awarded to customers who would be the first in their family to own a Buick.

There was no dickering on price. Those lucky enough to qualify paid full sticker plus a hefty premium. Hollywood celebrities, and even some of the same Arab sheiks whose embargo had rendered the gas-guzzlers worthless in the first place, were frantic now to obtain a Buick from Bridges's dealership. They were content, indeed grateful, to pay a surcharge for the privilege, plus a hefty fee to ship the auto abroad.

Some customers actually preferred to pay more rather than less. The higher price fulfilled their narcissism—the vehicle was worth more because they paid more.

"Thirty-eight thousand for your Electra?" California's Governor George Deukmejian was overheard bragging to reggae music pioneer Toots Hibbert at a Grammys after-party at the Hollywood Roosevelt Hotel. "Mine—identical model, identical options—ran me forty-two!"

With the trial now underway, first Ezra Convy, then both Bakers, and eventually Warren Robertson took the stand.

Each, in turn, recited a well-rehearsed litany of falsehoods.

"Dwight Bridges, the man sitting over there, our codefendant, he shows up for band practice as usual that night, with a gallon of moonshine in him, and another gallon in a jug in his hand, and some crazy scheme to 'do something,' as he put it, about this gas thing, this energy thing."

Ezra Convy paused to dwell on one particularly irksome aspect of Bridges's behavior that night.

"First, he tries to get me to slip him some gas," Convy told the court, "even though I'm closed, even though I'm trying, in the spirit of patriotism, to ration what little there is to my regular customers, decent, honest citizens of Hoggzswallow Hollow, and not a one of them, except Dwight, trying to squeeze favors from me, sir, judge, Your Honor."

Convy paused for a moment to catch his breath, and then he continued.

"He gets us all liquored up, piles us into his automobile, we don't have no idea where we're being took, and we only go along to try and see that our friend don't get into trouble. It's dark, see. The township's cut back on streetlights, what with the oil lumbago or whatever they call it. So we can't really see where we're at. Given all that's come down since, seems like it was that place, that Hebrew place, that Jew church, the sinner-agog, whatever they call it, where Dwight hands us spray-paint cans, see, and all we can do is try to talk him out of it while he goes on his silly little rampage, painting this, that, and the other thing."

Convy paused here once again.

He cleared his throat, took a sip of water, and sat in silence.

"Please proceed," the prosecutor instructed Convy.

"Dwight whips out a lighter and invites us to join him in burning the place to the ground. Thanks be to God in heaven, we muster the strength to restrain him. Still, each one of us feels foolish about it. Should have stopped him from the get-go. At the very least, we should have reported it to the authorities in—what do lawyers call it?—a timely fashion. But friends is friends. Me and my pals clearly suffered from some warped sense of backwoods loyalty."

Plea-bargainers Convy, Robertson, and the Bakers told the court that they experienced the deepest contrition: all of them, that is, except for the younger Baker, who experienced instead what he called "conniption," then tried "condition," finally settling on "contraption."

Throughout the boys' testimony, Bridges sat comfortably, even serenely, taking it all in. He processed the perjury without apparent resentment. He seemed almost pleased, even satisfied. Now and again he nodded and smiled at Convy and the others, though all averted their eyes.

Not to worry, Bridges's lawyer assured him at the lunch recess on the third day. Soon enough his turn would come, and he would tell the truth, he would report what had really transpired that night at the Jewish temple.

Faithful Buddy Scheib, occupying a seat in the front row, had retained for Bridges the fanciest of fancy-ass attorneys, a senior partner at the storied criminal-defense firm Garvey, Lopes, and Cey.

Conservatively suited but flaunting a feral coif calling to mind Cosmo Kramer, the lawyer reassured his client. These perjurers, he told Bridges, these Saltine crackers were as transparent as the glass on Dwight Bridges's back porch, the same glass they had smashed in their efforts to tamper with evidence. Their motivation for lying was manifest. Even this hillbilly judge and redneck jury, Bridges's lawyer predicted, would see through their lies.

And if for some reason they did not, victory would certainly be won on appeal.

Regarding his co-conspirators, Bridges calmed himself, recalling advice offered not by Yogi Berra but Western author Robert Hanlon: "Never ascribe to malice that which can be adequately explained by stupidity."

All the while, Bridges sat there quietly, Mother Bridges at his side. They seemed like strangers, the two of them, which is to say they seemed like a mother and her adult son.

Besides Bridges, there was but one other witness for the defense, half-deaf old Albert Morrow, who lived down the block from Convy's Mobil.

Morrow testified that he'd been kept awake that night by the band rehearsing into the early morning hours. That was long after Convy, the Bakers, and Robertson, according to their testimony, had observed Dwight Bridge's purported antics at Temple B'Nai Ohev Shalom, dabbling in some unsolicited exterior redecorating.

Morrow reported that he had heard Dixieland music blaring from Ez Convy's service bay at the same time Bridges was supposedly committing a hate crime across town. How could he have desecrated the synagogue when he was several miles away, at band rehearsal with Ez, the Bakers, and Warren Robertson?

Morrow's account would clear Bridges, his counsel assured him. "Nobody can be in two places at the same time."

Clearly, the attorney had never heard of the positron-emission muon ionic holographic tele-transporter.

"You'll take the stand," the lawyer told Bridges. "You'll utilize a tactic I call 'the old truth ploy.' You'll tell the truth. That's all you have to do. If you tell the truth, acquittal is a slam dunk."

The attorney babbled on throughout lunch, oozing confidence in anticipation of the trial's outcome. During this time, neither Bridges nor Mother Bridges spoke or ate. Not even Buddy Scheib could get a word past this big-city mouthpiece.

It was all fine by Bridges.

He closed his ears to the anxious chatter. He consulted with only his memory and his conscience.

What had truly happened that night at the synagogue? How had he been transported to Las Vegas?

Ez Convy was lying through his teeth, of course, along with the rest of them, but was he really such a bad ol' boy? Hadn't he provided Bridges with gas that night? And Warren Robertson? Clearly, he was not among your cerebral heavyweights, hardly the cherry in the Chuckles bar. That said, though, there was no denying he blew a wicked clarinet. At the end of the day, wasn't his heart in its assigned location, exactly where God put it?

As for the Bakers?

Well, the Bakers were the Bakers, that's all you could say about the Bakers. It must have hurt them to wallow in deception right there in front of Bridges, with Mother Bridges looking on.

The courtroom fell silent when he took the stand.

CHAPTER
4O

"No further questions," were the first and final words Bridges's lawyer said to him once the defendant was seated and sworn.

"But you haven't asked him any questions," the judge said.

"Your honor, ladies and gentlemen of the jury," the lawyer said with a flourish, "friends, countrymen, countrywomen, elders, stakeholders, and all the ships at sea," he continued, "my faith in this witness's veracity is so profound that I am content to turn him over immediately to hostile examination by the people's representative."

Here was the kind of surprise tactic upon which the lawyer's reputation was founded.

The judge shook his head slowly. "This is most irregular."

After a hefty pause, he nodded reluctantly to the prosecutor. "Proceed."

The district attorney was caught completely off guard, which was, of course, defense counsel's design. The prosecutor bent awkwardly over the table, pretending to review notes. Clearly, however, he was merely stalling for time, trying to think of something to say.

He rose unsteadily from his chair and approached the stand.

At long last, he said to the witness, "Would you please state your name for the record?"

Defense counsel leaped to his feet. "Objection!"

"You object to the witness stating his name for the record?" the judge said calmly, furrowing his brow just slightly, as if such stunts were a normative aspect of judicial protocol. Beneath the jurist's placid demeanor, however, one could sense a simmering furor.

"Yes, your honor," Bridges's lawyer said. "That is correct."

The judge spoke slowly now, deliberately, removing his glasses and wiping them with the gathered fringe of his robe. "Prior to my ruling," he said to the lawyer, "would you care to share with the court any grounds supporting your objection?"

In America, nobody "told" or "said" or "stated" or "declared" anything anymore. No one "asserted" or "suggested." No one "expressed" or "disclosed" or "maintained" or "mentioned" or "voiced" or "remarked" or "affirmed" or "averred" or "observed" or "divulged" or "revealed" anything.

In the newly corrupted vernacular, what everybody did now was "share."

"Grounds?" defense counsel asked, as if it were the first time he had ever heard the term, as if he had been absent from law school the day they taught that.

The judge nodded.

"Hearsay," the lawyer said.

"Hearsay?"

"Hearsay."

"Is there an echo in here?" Dwight Bridges might have asked had he been onstage at a club, clad in his Richie Ritchie persona.

Replacing his glasses on his face, the judge queried the defense counsel, "The defendant reporting his name for the record constitutes hearsay?"

"Absolutely right, Your Honor," the lawyer said. "How can he know his name, except for the fact that, however long ago, his parents told it to him? Testimony regarding his name relies solely upon information communicated to him by others. Isn't that the textbook definition of 'hearsay'? The defendant has no firsthand, empirically verifiable knowledge of his name. Nobody does. Our names are exclusively an inference each of us draws, based upon what other people say."

The judge's patience was clearly flagging. Lilac-hued veins swelled visibly beneath the surface of his hairless scalp, creating a pattern resembling routes on a roadmap. Clearly, the jurist struggled to restrain himself from erupting into a full-tilt tantrum.

The prosecutor stood there dumbfounded, viewing the proceedings as if he had stumbled into the courtroom by accident while surveilling the corridors in search of a water fountain, or restroom, or the self-serve sundries kiosk on the second-floor with its coffee-and-snacks vending machines.

"You suggest to the court that nobody on Earth knows their name?" the judge asked.

"Respectfully, Your Honor, counsel's purpose here is not to speculate on generalities pertaining to everybody on Earth but to determine precisely what sort of testimony is admissible in this court. We seek merely to explore issues related to this particular action, in this particular jurisdiction, regarding testimony offered by the particular witnesses appearing before the bench today."

The judge said, "Overruled."

A silence the size of Wyoming settled over the courtroom.

At last, the judge looked to the prosecutor. Struggling to mask his impatience, he grumbled, "Do you wish by any chance to resume your cross examination?"

The prosecutor came awake as from out of a coma. "Yes, yes," he said, blinking nervously. "Of course." He thought for a moment. "Where were we?"

"Dwight Bridges," Dwight Bridges said. "My name is Dwight Bridges."

The packed gallery tittered.

"Yes!" the prosecutor said brightly. "And could you tell us your occupation?"

"I'm a car dealer, Buicks, new and used, right here in Hoggzswallow Hollow …," Bridges said quickly, before his lawyer could lodge another objection.

Spectators in the gallery burst into belly-shaking laughter. Even the jury joined them now, shouting in unison, "… West Virginia!"

"Silence in the court!" the judge hollered, crashing his gavel on the bench, splintering the handle and sending the head flying across the room. "Dee-court room in the core-um!" he shouted, withdrawing a fresh gavel from a pocket deep in his robes, like a home-plate umpire supplying a pitcher with a fresh ball.

Clearly, the magistrate was a regular gavel-breaker.

For a moment, the judge sat still with a vacant expression on his face.

"Decorum in the court room," he said at last, revising his previous remark.

Again, he glared at the prosecutor.

Again, the prosecutor appeared startled from a deep stupor.

"I beg your pardon?" he asked the judge, rolling his shoulders, flexing his limbs, and rubbing his eyes, like Rip Van Winkle awakening from his twenty-year nap.

The judge turned to Bridges. "Have you ever utilized an alias?"

"Truth to tell, Your Honor," Bridges said, "the whole truth and nothing but, I have searched my mind and my memory and my conscience and my consciousness, and I have absolutely, positively no recollection of ever having used any name besides the one I just now stated."

Bridges paused thoughtfully.

"I acknowledge, however," he said, resuming his testimony, "that many people call me by another name. I have seen filmed images of someone who, though he has a full head of hair, claims my name as his own, not to mention also my occupation and hometown."

Again, the gallery and jury tittered. The judge silenced them with a fresh volley from his mallet.

"Let me put it this way—" the judge continued.

"Objection!" Bridges's lawyer was on his feet.

"But I haven't asked the question," the judge said.

"Our point precisely," the defense attorney explained. "Not the presiding judge, but examining counsel, asks the questions."

"Shuttup!" the judge commanded him.

"I'm prepared to resume my examination of the witness," the people's representative volunteered.

"Shuttup!" said the judge.

He turned back to face Bridges.

"Have you ever used the name 'Richie Ritchie'?"

"Your Honor, to the best of my recollection I have never used that name. Nevertheless, I acknowledge that it appears somehow to have been assigned to me."

"Assigned? By whom?"

"Beats me," Bridges said.

"All the same, I insist you answer the question. Is your name Dwight Bridges or is it Richie Ritchie?"

"Yes," Bridges said.

"Yes?"

"Yes, Your Honor."

"Yes what?" the judge barked, the vessels beneath his pate darkening now from periwinkle to plum. "I'll ask you one more time: Is your name Dwight Bridges or is it Richie Ritchie?"

"Yes," Bridges said again.

"Yes?" the judge echoed.

"Yes," Bridges said. "My name is Dwight Bridges or Richie Ritchie."

The court room erupted into laughter and cheers.

It took the jurist an additional pair of fractured gavels to restore order.

"I don't find that one bit funny," the judge said.

"Respectfully, Your Honor," Bridges's lawyer said, "people all across the nation find it funny. Downright hilarious is how they find it."

"I am especially pleased you make that point," the judge said with sarcasm so thick you could stir it with an oar. "As far as the court is concerned, if he is found guilty of these charges, your client can laugh his ass off all the way to jail. Humor is not the subject of this trial. And simply because we have a wide audience inside and outside this courtroom, and merely because we have costly counsel with show-business credentials, and an income larger than that of his superstar clients, I'll not allow this procedure to be turned into a sketch from *The Colgate Comedy Hour*."

Bridges recalled having seen kinescoped reruns of show on Channel 34.

"Tell us if you will," the people's counsel asked Bridges, "where were you on the night of ...," and he specified the date of the alleged trespass against the township's Jewish house of worship.

Savvy lawyers, of course, only ask questions to which they already know the answers. The state's attorney had prepared as best he could to rebut what Bridges's testimony would surely be, his shockproof, waterproof, ironclad alibi—that on the night in question, thousands had seen him in Las Vegas, Nevada, in the fabulous Starshine Dome of the phenomenal Desert Goliath Hotel, Country Club, Resort, Spa, and Casino.

Instead, Bridges said simply, "It was just like the boys told it."

There was so colossal an intake of breath in the courtroom that the air pressure palpably plunged, causing everyone's ears to pop.

"I was at my dealership," Bridges said. "I shut down operations for the night, brought up from the cellar a couple gallons of moonshine, chugged one all by myself, brought the other with me to Ez Convy's Mobil, just like Ez himself testified."

"May I approach the bench?" Bridges's attorney asked, seeking to stifle his own client's testimony.

But Bridges continued.

"By eleven thirty or midnight, I had the boys fairly blind with booze. From the way they were playing their instruments, I knew they were pretty far gone. Old Baker there, for instance, he was experiencing tempo issues, which isn't like him at all. He may not be a giant when it comes to social skills, but he's one heck of a piano player. Never misses a beat. When Old Baker tickles the ivory, you understand why piano is characterized not as a string instrument but percussion."

"Spare us the musicology lecture," the judge said. "Stick to the facts."

"I put a Dixieland tape on an eight-track cassette machine, turned it way up loud to play while we were away. Anybody in the neighborhood who heard it, for instance Albert Morrow over there, would think we were still rehearsing. I confess I thought it was pretty darn clever of me. Now, however, I realize it merely establishes my pre-meditation."

Bridges's lawyer settled quietly into his chair, his forehead beginning to glisten with sweat.

Ezra Convy, the Bakers, and Warren Robertson all looked at each other, shaking their heads in confusion and disbelief.

"I put the fellows in my car," Bridges continued, "and drove them over to the synagogue. They had no idea where they were going or what they were doing. The rest? It's exactly like you heard them tell it. They tried to stop me, but I spray-painted racist epithets on the temple. It was dumb, I admit it. I was angry, really in a bit of a panic, thanks to this gas thing, this energy thing, which was wrecking my business, ruining what I'd struggled for years to build up. The sheiks who embargoed the oil, who caused all this mess, they're so many miles away. I needed somebody to blame, somebody I could see, a target, a punching bag, a scapegoat. Isn't that the Jews' tradition, their heritage? They'll tell you so themselves. They're the world's leading blame-takers, everybody knows that. Wasn't our dear, sweet, precious Lord Jesus himself a Jew who took upon himself the burden of everybody else's sin?"

Bridges paused here to catch his breath.

The courtroom reverberated with a deafening silence. All that was missing was the dropping of a pin.

Bridges picked up the thread.

"Throughout the millennia," he said, "Jews have lived their lives peering over their shoulders for Cossacks, Nazis, the Klan. If bigots like me aren't haunting, taunting, and stalking them, they're almost disappointed."

Bridges sat quietly for a moment.

"As for this Richie Ritchie business," he said, "I can't explain it. Isn't each and every one of us many different people all at the same time? A single person can be both a parent and a child. A grandparent and a grandchild. An uncle and a nephew. An aunt and a niece. A lover and a hater. A friend and an enemy. A performer and an observer. A buyer and a seller. Myself, as soon as I grow the least bit angry or afraid, I become someone else, a completely different person, like that comic-book character—what do they call him?—the Hulk."

Here Bridges paused.

"On the evening in question," he continued, "I was frightened. I was resentful. Fear combined with stupidity, that's bigotry. It's a lethal mix. I'm lucky all that happened is that I was placed in the

body of some other fellow, apparently this Richie Ritchie character, at another time, in some other place."

Bridges sat quietly for a moment.

He took out his hanky and mopped his brow.

"Why does it matter how it happened?" Bridges said. "We can
wonder about it from now until, say, Flag Day, whenever that is.
What's certain is that I acted wrongfully. I don't only admit that. I
don't merely acknowledge or concede it. I assert it. I proclaim it."

He indicated Convy and the others.

"These good ol' boys here, they had nothing to do with what
went down that night. For that, I take full credit."

Now neither Bridges nor anybody else said anything at all.

Finally, the judge spoke up. "Court is recessed for twenty
minutes."

Exercising uncharacteristic restraint, the jurist rapped his gavel,
this time most delicately.

All the same, the mallet shattered into a thousand pieces.

CHAPTER
41

Nischt geferlekh, Bridges thought to himself. *It's no tragedy.*
Pleading down his charges to Malicious Mischief, Disorderly Conduct, and Disturbing the Peace, Bridges pulled four and a half months in the minimum-security state honor farm outside of Martinsburg.

How he had come to know Yiddish was a total mystery.

Fluency had emerged out of the blue. His vocabulary included far more than the familiar terms that had migrated over the years into everyday English, like *chutzpah, schlep,* or *kvetch.* In the humble prison library, when he had stumbled upon Isaac Bashevis Singer's *Der Spinozist* in the original Yiddish, he read it from cover to cover, not once but twice.

Beyond the time in jail, the judge imposed also a five-hundred-dollar fine, which he promptly suspended.

For Bridges, the money would have been no problem. Thanks to acclaim resulting from the trial, business on Old Deerfield was booming. With the oil crisis still not wholly abated, few regular folks were purchasing gas-guzzling 1974 Buicks. Still, any car bearing the license-plate frame reading *Bridges Buick of Hoggzwallow Hollow* had acquired a cachet.

In the spirit of reconciliation, and to ease his conscience, in lieu of the suspended fine Bridges contributed five hundred dollars to the Temple B'Nai Ohev Shalom building fund.

In the interim, among instruments stored in a cupboard that were part of the prison's music-therapy rehabilitative program, Bridges discovered a workable Etude ETR-100 Series Bb horn. Soon enough he found himself jamming with a couple of Black inmates up from Yazoo City, Mississippi, serving time for check-kiting and bunko. One blew a mournful sax; the other stroked a wicked country fiddle. They were Bridges's colleagues not only musically but also at their jobs in the prison laundry. Their fellow jailbirds clearly relished the trio's performances at the regularly scheduled Thursday night talent shows.

Mother Bridges routinely sent care packages, which Bridges distributed entirely among the members of his newfound incarcerated family. This was no act of generosity. He would not have said so aloud but, notwithstanding a bounty of virtues, Mother was a dreadful cook.

To Bridges, by comparison, the prison fare was epicurean.

During his brief tenure in the slammer, he gained eight pounds.

In obeisance to early release protocols, plus time off for good behavior, after serving fifteen weeks, Bridges was sprung.

Upon returning home, it was clear to him that things were not the same in Hoggzswallow Hollow. In no time at all, cable had transmogrified the social and cultural landscape. Every household now had a television set. Folks were dizzy to distraction with the host of channels, the seemingly limitless inventory of entertainment options, the deluge of information alternatives that had become accessible.

With a multitude of virtual families now at hand—Bradys, Bunkers, Partridges, and Ewings, not to mention Laverne, Shirley, plus Sanford and Sanford's son—a fickle public seemed to lose all recollection of a comedian named Richie Ritchie.

The virtuosi with whom Bridges had collaborated in jail had spoiled him forever as far as dilettantes like the Bakers, Warren Robertson, and Ez Convy were concerned. Upon his release, Bridges quit the Dixieland band. He sold the Buick franchise and vanished somewhere out west.

Nobody in Hoggzswallow Hollow knew precisely where.

CHAPTER
42

It was a mescaline sunset.

Neon-fringed cirrus clouds lent an art-deco aspect to the New Mexico twilight. Indigo patches of sky laced with lavender faded to slate, then to eggplant purple, the color of a bruise. Bottom-lit cumulonimbus formations, tinged by strata as pink as Pepto-Bismol, lay stacked upon one another above the horizon like bolts of fabric arrayed on the shelves of a textile emporium.

If Kodak had processed this image and returned the film to the photographer, it would have been resubmitted to the lab for what Hollywood technicians call Color Correction.

Dwight Bridges paid no attention to the sunset. He watched instead the local newscast and grumbled about the latest gas crisis.

Deciding whom to hate the most was a toss-up: this Ayatollah fellow who had just ousted the Shah guy and was provoking a passel of trouble in the region, or the local TV weather dude, a prancing, practicing, card-carrying wuss name of Wilbur Morton. He seemed somehow familiar to Bridges, though he couldn't quite place him.

In a locale such as Gallup, Bridges told himself, the weather's pretty much the same every day. Still, this Wilbur guy managed to screw up each and every forecast.

Bridges considered writing a letter to the station.

He didn't write a letter to the station.

Instead, he pulled himself up out of his chair and made his way through his adobe bungalow, double-bolting each and every window, preparing to go out and make his rounds. Used to go out, he mused mournfully, without even closing the door, let alone locking it.

But that was before.

That was before the nation had gone whole-hog haywire, before there was crime at every street corner in every city, before this newest gas thing, this latest energy thing. Here and now, in '79, with the Iranian Revolution underway and the consequent disruption of oil supplies, gas lines were even worse than anybody remembered from the Middle Eastern crisis six years earlier, the previous time Americans had found themselves waiting in queues for their fill-up.

In an effort to conserve fuel, Bridges maintained a feather-light foot on the accelerator, as if there were a raw egg between the sole of his shoe and the pedal. Driving in this manner, Bridges headed for the first location, his unit on Paseo Mendoza between Boardman Avenue and Old Route 66.

Turning onto Mission, he caught sight of an open Shell with a relatively short line, maybe three and a half blocks. It was too good to pass up, so Bridges hung a U-turn, swung in behind the last car, and killed the motor.

He waited.

As he waited, his blood began to boil. This trip shouldn't be necessary. In the old days, his several locations could operate unattended all night, twenty-four hours, seven days, fifty-two weeks.

Hadn't that been the idea?

Waiting in line for gas, he worried that before he reached the pumps they would run dry. Sitting there behind the wheel, however, he rationalized that the one thing he had in plentiful supply was time.

Time to ruminate.

When he had unloaded his auto dealership back East years earlier, he'd endeavored to swap it for a turnkey enterprise in a distant state, some sort of venture that would manage itself. He had sought an enterprise with a reliable cash flow, however modest, that would not require too much time and attention.

His introduction to the professional laundry sector had arisen out of his stint in prison, where he had worked the washing machines in collaboration with a pair of incarcerated Black musicians.

Bridges brooded.

What had gone wrong?

Everything, that's what.

This dad-blamed permissiveness, this lax attitude on the part of everybody, especially the young people. The breakdown of family values, of decent, patriotic, old-fashioned American precepts and principles. Years earlier, when he'd first relocated to the Southwest, the Mexicans and the Indians, they kept to themselves, they knew their place. No more. The Hispanics and Native Americans, as they now had to be called, were sitting in, acting out, and just generally making trouble.

The line moved slowly.

Each time it did, Bridges started his engine, drove one car length forward, then turned it off.

After only forty-five minutes, the blink of an eye these days for a gas line, he was stationed beside the pump, watching the tawny, pockmarked teenage attendant insert the hose.

The car took eighteen cents worth of gas before the pump shut down with a metallic click.

"What is this?" the Zuni youth said, inspecting the equipment. "Say," he said, "look here. You're full up. Eighteen cents fills you to the brim. You were full when you drove in here."

"I must have misread my gauge," Bridges lied.

"Why do you waste my time? You got a full tank, and you wait in line an hour waiting for a fill-up? Christ-a-mighty, what's up with people these days?"

Used to be you came in for gas, Bridges recollected, and you got crisp, efficient service. They were glad to see you, grateful for your trade. You drove right up to the pump. They checked the oil, you never had to ask. They scrubbed your glass, front and rear, even your lights and exterior mirrors. They sponsored contests, ran games, distributed green stamps, offered jackpots, sweep-stakes, prizes. It was a fun place, a gas station. Now what do you get? A lot of know-nothing smart-lip attitude, a metric ton of disrespect from some arrogant, snot-nosed, jerk-brained, half-wit, half-breed punk.

Bridges worried that it was only a matter of time before drivers would be required to pump their own gas. He derived some solace, however, knowing that American motorists would never tolerate an injustice so degrading as that.

"Listen, you," the attendant reprimanded Bridges, "don't come in here again with a full tank. Instead of stupid, try smart."

"Must have misread my gauge," Bridges lied again. He reached into his pocket and pulled out a quarter. He handed it to the attendant.

"Jesus, Mary, and Joseph," the attendant said, fishing for change. "If people weren't so damned greedy," he complained, his voice loud enough to be heard across the state in Las Cruces, "maybe we could get by. But pimps like you, true bozos, they come in here and wait in line five hours, and the whole time they already have a full tank."

Trembling with irritation, Bridges climbed back into the car.

To hell with a light foot; Bridges floored the pedal. Forfeiting the seven pennies change, his Chevy Impala sped off, producing a high-pitched yip of tires and leaving behind the stench of burnt rubber.

Steeped in rage bordering on apoplexy, Bridges tore down Mission, blowing through one light after another. Now, somewhere deep in his cortex, circuits kicked in, and he realized he was on the road to annihilation. In response, he steered hard right, turned up a dim side street, and lurched to a halt at the curb outside a dark mom-'n'-pop liquor outlet. A sign on the door informed customers that, in keeping with newly mandated federal energy-conservation protocols, the establishment had closed early.

Bridges switched off the headlights and killed the motor.

Holding his head in his hands, he rocked back and forth where he sat, swaying and shuddering in place behind the wheel, as if seized by convulsions. What's happening to me? he asked himself. What's happening to my country?

He took several deep breaths.

Gotta pull myself together, get over to the locations and collect the proceeds, he told himself. If I don't clear the machines and lock down the units, the Latinos and Indigenous Peoples will loot the coin boxes and burn the establishment to the ground.

He was still too rattled, however, to resume driving. He stepped from the car and leaned against the driver's door, struggling to catch his breath and regain his composure.

And then he saw it.

Opposite him, across Molina, was a rented storefront with a hand-lettered notice taped to the door. Scrawled with a Sharpie

on a shirt cardboard from the dry cleaners, the sign bore the legend
Centro De La Raza—Chicano Community Clinic Coalition—Food
Stamp Applications and Free Medical Services.

The facility was closed for the night.

An eerie calm settled over Bridges.

He looked up and down the dimly lit lane. In keeping with
federal energy policy, only every third streetlamp was aglow.

A thought crossed his mind.

He got back into the car, reached into the glove compartment,
fished around blindly, and came up with, of all things, a lipstick.

How'd a lipstick get in here? he wondered. Perhaps it had been
left there by the car's previous owner.

Emerging from the vehicle, Bridges peered up and down the
deserted street, reassuring himself that he was alone. Cautiously,
he slinked across to the opposite curb. He crept up to the establishment's front door. He removed the cap from the lipstick and
turned the screw.

A crimson stub protruded from the tip.

In block letters, upon the door he scrawled: *"WETBACK*
PEPPER-GUTS SWIM HOME!!!"

Again, he looked up and down the street.

He tossed the lipstick.

His affect gone wholly flat, with a vacant expression on his face,
he crouched down low and dislodged a loose paving stone from
the cobbled roadbed. He hefted it to his shoulder and heaved it
through the plate-glass window.

He climbed back into the car and drove away.

At the corner of Lagoda, he switched on the car's radio.

KGLX-AM talk-show host Bobby Bones was commiserating
in Spanglish with an Anglo caller despairing over the abduction
of diplomats from the American embassy in Teheran. A defiant
Bridges, now deliberately seeking to waste fuel, switched on the

air conditioner full blast, even though Gallup's autumnal evening temperature was a nippy fifty-two.

A pair of right turns took him back to Mission.

At last he arrived at his location, a storefront featuring a sign that read *Econo-Wash LaundraMatic Free Dry*.

He watched impatiently as a squat, acne-scarred Hopi extracted her laundry from a dryer while her litter of brats chased each other around the premises, weaving up and back among the machines, squealing, screaming, and scuffing up the equipment. He waited while she collected her clothes and her offspring, and departed the harshly lit establishment.

Bridges double-bolted the door.

He reversed the placard hanging there so that it now read CLOSED.

He moved from machine to machine, unlocking the coin boxes and pouring the change into the canvas bag provided by Pinnacle Bank.

Not much of a haul, he reckoned, hefting the sack. It was easy to understand why the takes were diminishing. This energy thing. The Mexicans. The Indians. They couldn't find gas, couldn't afford it at today's prices—nearly a dollar gallon—even when they could find it. So they stayed home and wallowed in their squalor.

In the rare instance they laundered anything, they did so by hand in the kitchen sink.

Or in the toilet, Bridges groused in silence.

Now the government was threatening to compel him and all merchants to ration their electrical power. What was he to do? Unplug the machines? Go out of business altogether? Roll over and goddamn die?

What a wave of folly was sweeping the land!

He carried the bank collections bag around back and dropped it into the floor safe.

Next, he moved to the junction box on the rear wall.

He swung open the panel door, revealing twin ranks of electrical switches.

One at a time, he threw the switches, turning off the lights.

As he did so, the place grew progressively darker.

At last, there remained but a single switch.

He turned it off.

Instead of plunging into darkness, however, the enterprise came aglow in a torrent of incandescence.

Odd, he thought. What do you know about that?

He took a second swipe at the switch, but his hand raked air—the switch was gone. Not only the switch, but the junction box, the wall itself, the machines, the whole dang laundromat.

Darndest thing.

Somewhere in the background, a Norteño combo played "Rinconcito en el Cielo." Trumpets giggled and sobbed. An ample-bellied guitarrón thumped and plunked. Scattered picante accordion triplets dusted the melody like powdered sugar on a tray of churros.

Bridges assumed the music had to be coming from some gang-banger cholo strutting down the street, his boom box blaring.

There was a sharp rapping at the door.

"One minute, Señor Ricardo!" a voice called out. "Your cue! Señor Ricardo? Are you ready? One minute!"

What the hey? Bridges muttered to himself, dipping a powder-puff into a cylinder containing foundation the color of café-au-lait. He patted his cheekbones and forehead, striving to dampen the highlights gleaming back at him from the mirror.

Mission Statement

Heresy Press promotes freedom, honesty, openness, dissent, and real diversity in all of its manifestations. We discourage authors from descending into self-censorship, we don't blink at alleged acts of cultural appropriation, and we won't pander to the presumed sensitivities of hypothetical readers. We also don't judge works based on the author's age, gender identity, racial affiliation, political orientation, culture, religion, non-religion, or cancellation status. Heresy Press's ultimate commitment is to enduring quality standards, i.e. literary merit, originality, relevance, courage, humor, and aesthetic appeal.

Newsletter

Don't miss the Heresy Press Newsletter SPEAKEASY:
https://heresy-press.com/newsletter

Other Heresy Press Titles

Nothing Sacred: Outspoken Voices in Contemporary Fiction
The Hermit by Katerina Grishakova
Animal by Alan Fishbone
Unsettled States by Tom Casey
Devil Take It by Daniel Debs Nossiter